32 Minutes

Andrew Diamond

Cover design by Lindsay Heider Diamond.

ISBN (Paperback): 978-1734139273
ISBN (Kindle): 978-1734139280

PRAISE FOR GATE 76
Freddy Ferguson #1

A consummate thriller with some of the best characterization you'll see all year. — Kirkus Reviews (starred review)

Gate 76 is about loss and redemption... [Freddy Ferguson] doesn't see his own goodness, the spark of caring that sets him apart from his brutal upbringing... Freddy doesn't believe in much of anything, not even justice. He does believe in following his instincts and doing the right thing, even when it may lead to his destruction. — Sharon Vander Meer, One Roof Publishing

One of the year's best thrillers. — BestThrillers.com

A phenomenal mystery novel with dynamic characters and a gripping and intricate plot. — Susan Sewell, Readers' Favorite

PRAISE FOR KILL ROMEO
Freddy Ferguson #2

A fast-paced, first-rate murder mystery that crackles with sexual tension… entertaining, suspenseful and cathartic. — BestThrillers.com

A thrilling page-turner… To say Andrew Diamond knows how to spin a thriller of a story is an understatement. — The Feathered Quill

Ferguson is deeply relatable thanks to Diamond's elaboration of his inner life, which matches the intrigue of the murder mystery at the heart of the story. — The BookLife Prize

1

My first impression of Leighton Graham? The man didn't like anyone but himself, and he may even have been on the fence about that.

Which made him perfect for his job. The board of directors of a publicly traded company called Recursion Talent had hired him as CEO to turn around an ailing company. That meant slash-and-burn layoffs and ruthless cost cutting, all of which was inflicted on workers he would never meet.

The cuts and the austerity program didn't apply to the executive suite. Graham's spacious office on the top floor of a building in Reston Town Center was furnished in cherrywood and black leather, with museum-lit modern paintings and sculptures, and huge west-facing windows through which he looked down on the world.

He was in his early fifties with short grey hair, neatly trimmed. Tailored suit, light blue with yellow tie, Italian leather designer shoes, six foot one or two, and obsessively fit. The kind of guy who's in the gym at 5:00 a.m. and does the full weight circuit in exactly one hour, without a second wasted between sets.

Two hours earlier, his assistant, Nettie Hernandez, had asked me to come out to the office ASAP. I did. Made it in just over an hour from DC, and then spent forty-five minutes waiting on the couch in reception before Graham emerged from his office, looked me up and down with a scowl of disapproval and said, "This the guy?"

"This is Mr. Ferguson," his assistant said. "The investigator."

"Send him in."

Then he turned and disappeared into his office.

I stood, slid my phone into my pocket, and entered the office to find Graham walking from a side table to his desk with a manila envelope in hand. He didn't ask me to sit, just tossed the envelope on the desk and said nothing.

"What's this?" I asked.

"Your job. What's your email, Mr. Ferguson?"

I told him. He leaned over his desk and typed it into his laptop and said, "I'm cc'ing you." On what, he didn't say.

He turned and stood at the window watching the big passenger jets descend across the snaking highway into Dulles Airport.

I opened the envelope and slid the contents into my right hand. A photo of a middle-aged man. Blond hair, pale blue eyes, grey suit, and red tie. It looked like a profile picture from a corporate website.

"Find him," said Graham.

I read the fact sheet. Karl Larsson was the Chief Technology Officer of Recursion Talent, leading their Artificial Intelligence initiative. His home was twenty minutes from the office. He was married with two kids, both college age.

I had heard about this case on the morning news, though I had been only half-listening and hadn't connected him to this company until now. He'd gone missing two days earlier. The cops were on it, but with no sign of foul play, they probably weren't working it too hard. If the guy ran off with his mistress, the case would solve itself soon enough.

A credit card charge would show up in Bali or Rome or Chicago. The Fairfax County cops would contact local law enforcement to make sure it was Larsson who had actually made the charge. They'd find out where he was staying, maybe even dig up the identity of his lady friend, and tell his wife it was a private matter for her and her lawyers.

"Do you know where he was last seen?" I asked. "And when?"

"Why don't you ask his wife?" Graham was abrupt and unpleasant.

"Do you *want* to find this guy?" I asked. "Because you're not being very helpful."

"What do you mean, do I *want* to find him? He's my CTO. I'm trying to run a damn company here. I got his wife crying in my ear and his whole tech team worried and distracted. They're not getting anything done. How much do you think that costs me each day? Find the guy, okay?"

Graham wasn't the type to charm people into getting what he wanted. His attitude was clear. I was hired help. I would do what he said because he was going to pay me.

And he was right. It was August, always a slow season in DC, and we were hurting for cash. I wanted my team to get paid, even if the money had to come from someone like this. I'd dealt with clients like him before. I tuned them out, focused on the job.

"You know if this guy Larsson had any reason to flee?" I asked. "Did he have a girlfriend on the side? Debts? Enemies?"

"You're the detective. You figure it out."

Graham made no effort to hide his condescension. His tone told me Larsson's disappearance was an inconvenience, like a puddle of puke someone had left on the floor, and I was the janitor who was supposed to clean it up.

"You have a contract?" he asked.

I pulled a folded contract from my jacket pocket, the standard terms we give every client, with a blank for the rates— retainer, my daily charge, and hourly rates for the rest of the team.

I leaned on his desk as I penned in the numbers, double what we normally charged. Then I quoted the rates aloud, half-hoping he would balk, so I could walk away from this one.

Anyone who's worked in a service industry learns soon enough that some clients aren't worth the trouble. But then, where else was I going to find work when the whole city was on vacation?

"I'll have my lawyer review that," Graham said. "And we'll be adding a clause." He didn't even look at the papers, just at me, sizing me up the way I used to size up opponents in the ring before a fight.

"You're adding a clause to the contract?"

That look, that sizing up—I knew it well. When I practiced it myself, sometimes the question behind it was, How much trouble is this guy going to give me? Other times, I knew at a glance my opponent was weak, doubting, outclassed. The question then was quicker, crueler, more dismissive. How quickly can I get rid of this guy?

The question I saw in Graham was the latter.

"You are to report to me at the end of each day," he said.

"I write a daily report," I told him, "and we keep it on file in the office. I give clients updates on major milestones, like when we get a break, or when we can definitively rule out—"

"I said you will report to me daily, at six p.m., in this office." He tapped his finger on the desk to emphasize the word *this*.

"That's not how it works," I said.

"That *is* how it works, Mr. Ferguson. It'll be in the contract. I'm not interested in milestones. You will tell me every detail. Everywhere you've been, everyone you've spoken to, everything you've learned, every day. Now stop wasting time and do your job."

It's not easy for a person to get under my skin, but this guy was doing it.

"Go ahead and put in your addendum," I said. "Sign it and get it back to me in an hour. I'll review it, and if I don't like it, I'm out."

I wasn't going to put more than sixty minutes into this case without a contract. I'd have Claire review it when it came in— she understood legalese better than I did—and if she didn't like it, we'd walk and let this guy find someone else.

I turned and left without a word.

Graham called after me, "I'll see you at six," his tone matter-of-fact, confident, an assertion of dominance.

As I rode the elevator down, my phone chimed. An email from Graham, addressed to all Recursion employees.

I'm sure by now you've heard the distressing news about our beloved CTO, Karl Larsson. Rest assured, Karl's safety is my first concern, and I will not rest until he returns safely.

I wasn't convinced of that. Graham didn't seem too concerned.

I have retained the services of world-class investigators to help locate Karl...

Actually, he had retained the services of one investigator, and I wouldn't call myself world-class, whatever that means. I just work hard.

It was interesting, though, to see how the CEO spun it. He understood what his audience wanted to hear, and he laid it on thick. Leighton Graham was a caring, stand-up guy who was on top of the situation.

I deleted the email without bothering to read the rest.

When I called Larsson's wife on the way out of the garage, she answered on the first ring. I told her who I was, who hired me.

"Can I come by and ask you some questions?"

"Yes." She sounded relieved. "Yes, please." Edgy and tense and grateful that someone was coming to help.

Her gratitude was the antidote to Graham's arrogance. This was why I was taking the job. Because there was always someone on the wrong end of a case like this, someone who's been blindsided, whose life has been upended, who's too distraught to know which way to turn.

2

As I drove along Reston Parkway, I called Leon and got some background on Graham's company. Leon had been digging into it since I left the office in DC.

Recursion Talent recruited employees for corporations around the world, specializing in high-paying and hard-to-fill positions. They also sold a suite of human resources software to thousands of large and medium-size companies.

Leon called their product "surveillance ware." He said it tracked everything employees did, every minute of the day. Their movements around the office, what they typed into their computer terminals, which websites they visited. It all went into central databases, giving managers an instant view into employee productivity, and flagging workers automatically for promotion consideration or disciplinary review.

That was one of the features they touted. In most organizations, you need a long trail of documented abuses before you can fire someone. Recursion's software built the trail for you, every minute of every day.

After they recruited you, surveilled you, demoted you, and fired you, their software's "exit module" would match you up with open positions at other companies and get you on the road to your next interview. Recursion earned a finder's fee for placing you in your new position. A few hundred of those paid for a new modernist painting on Leighton Graham's office wall, and you were right back on their hamster wheel, your life and career managed end-to-end by a machine.

"Now they're working on artificial intelligence," Leon said. "Like, they build a profile on you to match you up with a job."

"That's what Larsson was working on," I said. "Their new AI. I guess that's where everything is going these days. You find anything on Larsson?"

"He's from California," Leon said. "Moved to Virginia a few years ago. He has some court records related to a car accident. I'm still digging."

"All right. I'm getting close to his place. I'll check in later. And tell Claire I want her to look at this contract. This Graham guy has some special needs."

"Will do, Champ."

3

My first thought on reaching Larsson's address was this had to be the wrong house. Recursion Talent was a big company, publicly traded on the New York Stock Exchange, with over four billion in annual revenues. I imagined their Chief Technology Officer would pull in three hundred thousand a year, maybe even half a million. How could he live in a dump like this? In this little nineteen-eighties house with mildew-stained vinyl siding and a crabgrass yard?

The neighborhoods I drove past to get here were lined with million-dollar homes. This one, with its modest decades-old houses, was a big step down. This couldn't be right.

I parked in front, went up the concrete walk, sections of which had been pushed up by the roots of a sickly oak, and rang the bell. The woman who answered wasn't what I was expecting. With the name Larsson, I had pictured a fair-skinned, blue-eyed Swede, like Karl. I forgot she had married into this name.

She had dark brown hair, olive skin, and dark eyes that in youth might have shone with life. Beneath the current expression of worry, her face had a look of long endurance, as if years of hardship had taught her neither to hope nor fear, but simply to accept what came.

She wore a plain blue cotton skirt and black scoop-neck shirt that might have come from Old Navy.

"Mrs. Larsson?" I still wasn't sure this was the right house.

"Thank you for coming," she said, stepping back from the door to let me in.

Inside, the open door to the left showed an office with two computer monitors, a stack of books, and piles of mail strewn across a desk.

"Would you like some coffee? Or tea?"

"Coffee would be great."

She led me to the kitchen, straight back at the rear of the house. The living room we passed along the way was clean and uncluttered. Her space, at odds with the messy office that I assumed belonged to her missing husband. The dual monitors on the desk told me it was a techie's setup.

The kitchen, with its linoleum floor and Formica countertop, hadn't been updated since the house was built, probably in the early eighties. She kept it clean and tidy, and the sunlight streaming through the window above the sink kept the place from feeling cramped and depressing.

"So you met Leighton?" Erica Larsson scooped a tablespoon of ground coffee from a bulk-size Costco can and dumped it into the coffee maker. "What did you think of him?"

Normally, I won't speak ill of a person behind their back, but I make an exception for arrogant, unapologetic assholes. "I don't care for the guy."

"Neither do I. It always surprised me that Karl got along with him. On a professional level, I should say. He did Karl a favor by hiring him, and we were both grateful for that."

She added three more scoops to the coffee maker and then started filling the carafe with tap water.

"We didn't socialize, though," she explained. "Karl saw enough of him at work, and I, like you, don't care for him."

She cut the tap and poured the water into the coffee maker. "Leighton doesn't really talk to people anyway," she added. "Except when he wants something from them."

I'm glad we had both come to the same opinion of the man. That told me I wasn't letting my personal distaste get in the way of my judgment.

"If you don't mind me asking, why do you think he hired me? I mean, he's not the most caring guy."

"Pressure from above and below," she said, turning to face me. "The company brought him in a year and a half ago to turn things around. That's corporate-speak for laying off a quarter of the staff and making the remaining employees work unpaid overtime to pick up the slack. You see why he's the perfect person for that?

"A normal person would feel remorse for cutting off the livelihood of thousands of families, but Leighton only sees the bottom line. He's incapable of remorse, and most other human emotions as well. You know, I once had a dream he was in hell and the devil got frustrated because even the devil couldn't make him feel anything. Do you like milk in your coffee?"

"Sure."

She pulled a carton from the fridge and squinted at it.

"Sorry. This is expired. We have soy milk. Will that do?"

"Soy milk is fine."

She left the carton on the counter as the coffee maker chugged along.

"Back to your question about why Leighton would hire you. He's not well liked within the company. Karl is. I think the board of directors might have pressured Leighton to take action so he would look like he cared. That would score some points with the staff, that the boss was actually doing the right thing for once. The compassionate, humane thing."

We moved to the table at the end of the kitchen. I don't know what to call that area. It was too big to be a breakfast nook, and too small to be a dining room.

My phone chimed. A text from Leighton Graham telling me to check my email. He had sent a signed contract with his custom addendum insisting I report to him in person each day. I forwarded it to Claire and Ed with a message to review the addendum to make sure there were no legal tricks. I wasn't going to sign my soul away to this guy.

Matter of fact, I noted, *review the entire contract. Make sure his lawyer didn't slip anything else in there, or alter any of our boilerplate agreement.*

Claire texted right back. *You really think he'd sneak something in? You trust the guy that little?*

Yes, and yes, I replied.

Okay. I'll give it a close read.

I turned my attention back to Erica. "Sorry about that. Do you mind if I start with a few questions?"

She sat across from me, one of those people who looks you directly in the eye when you speak. Coming from a less compassionate spirit, that kind of attention could be unnerving. From her, it conveyed a simple generosity. You were her guest, and you had the whole of her attention.

"Please," she said. "Ask away."

"Did your husband have any enemies? Anyone he feared?"

She shook her head.

"Was he seeing anyone else?"

"Not that I know of."

"Not that you know of," I repeated, "but could he possibly have been seeing anyone?"

She hesitated, her eyes sweeping involuntarily across the table as she thought. Finally, "I don't think so."

"But you're not sure?"

She shook her head, no.

"Why aren't you sure? Why did you pause when I asked?"

She took a deep breath, let it out, and then looked me in the eye. "We haven't been very intimate this past year. I mean, we go through our phases, but usually he's affectionate with me. I know he's been under a lot of stress, and in the past, that's made him draw back a little. He's not as attentive to me when his mind is deep in work. But that usually passes as big projects come to completion."

The coffee maker began to rumble as the last of the water sputtered through. Erica got up and pulled two cups from the cabinet.

"A normal couple," she said as she poured a cup from the carafe, "would blow off steam by going out. You know, to dinner, or a movie or a play. Or they'd take a vacation, get away from the source of the stress, reset and reconnect."

She was starting to touch on the subject I was still trying to figure out how to approach. Why would a guy making hundreds of thousands a year be living like this? Did they not go out like a *normal couple* because they couldn't afford it? Where was all the money going?

Erica added soy milk to both cups and carried them to the table.

"I don't think he ran off with any woman," she said. "And I don't think he had any enemies. He wasn't scared of anyone that I know of."

"Ok," I said. I knew the next question would hurt, and I wasn't quite sure how to phrase it, so I just put it out there, bare and raw. "Do you think he'd run away to skip out on his debts?"

That one hit her in the gut. I could see it.

"God, I hope not," she said. "I truly hope he wouldn't do that. I mean, after all we've been through together. He would never have made it without me, and I wouldn't have made it without him. All these years, I've held on to this thread of hope, this certainty in the goodness of people despite their flaws, despite what they do and what happens with them. I've instilled it in our kids, and if he were to walk out and abandon me— Well that would be the end of my faith in people."

She told me Karl had been a promising young developer in Silicon Valley when they married in their twenties. By age twenty-nine, he was managing a team and earning good money. By thirty-two, they had two sons. And then, at thirty-eight, the accident.

"He'd been using cocaine," she said. "I knew about that. I thought it was a party thing. A once-a-month remnant left over from his twenties when he and the other coders worked seventy-hour weeks and wanted to stay awake long enough on a Friday night to go out and have some semblance of a social life.

"But he was using more than I knew. Daily, or almost daily, to keep on top of work. One evening after work—it was a Thursday, around ten p.m., and he'd just left the office—he was speeding along a road in Mountain View. He never thought he was speeding, not when he did coke. He hit another car and was badly injured.

"The two in the other car got it even worse. They both went on disability after the wreck, and Karl was on the hook for damages.

"We had money then, enough to hire a top lawyer who kept Karl out of jail. The lawyer's fees for the criminal case ran over a hundred thousand. We paid even more out of pocket for Karl's medical bills, and that was *after* insurance.

"We lost both civil suits—and we deserved it, I might add. We've been paying off the judgments ever since. Karl's salary might look impressive on paper, but we're supporting three families. Ours, and the families of the two people he injured. That's all garnished from his wages, by court order. And we have two sons in college now, and four parents in assisted living. We've been living hand-to-mouth for years."

"Why didn't you declare bankruptcy?"

"What's the point? You can't discharge claims from a DUI, even in bankruptcy. We just soldiered on."

She told me Karl had cleaned himself up after the crash. He never touched coke again. He barely even drank beer.

The family moved east a few years ago.

"It was too painful to stay there, after all we'd lost. It was painful for his victims too. We'd run into them and... And we just wanted to leave and start over."

They came to the DC area, where there were plenty of tech jobs and no one knew about his accident. Karl started over as a senior developer and worked his way up through management, which he didn't like.

"He liked to write code and design software systems," Erica told me. "But he needed the higher salary of the management positions. He kept working his way up. And then when Leighton took over at Recursion Talent, Leighton brought him on board as an executive."

The two had known each other in the Valley, she told me. Graham had been the CEO of a tech company that raised millions in venture capital and then went bust. Karl had been one of his top engineers.

Graham too had moved east after burning bridges in the Valley. No one could tolerate that abrasive personality for long. The guy was the corporate equivalent of the malignant narcissist every woman seems to have met on Tinder. The charm campaign that ends in abuse. After a while, his reputation precedes him. The victim pool dries up and he has to go somewhere else, where no one knows who he is.

Now Graham and Karl Larsson were both in Virginia, working together again. According to Erica, Graham liked Karl because Karl got things done reliably, on time, and with little fuss. I could see how that would appeal to an impatient CEO who wants his subordinates to make problems go away.

Karl's biggest project was an artificial intelligence engine that helped match highly skilled job candidates to high-paying positions. It was Recursion's "secret sauce" that led to a high retention rate among their recruits and lots of return business from satisfied customers.

"Okay," I said. "So, pardon me for saying this, but the more we can rule out up front, the better I can focus on productive avenues of investigation. You two have lived under heavy debt for many years. You haven't got to enjoy the fruits of your labor, and there's no sign of you ever getting out from under this debt."

I saw a little spark in her, like she was going to say something, but I went on and finished my point.

"That's a lot for anyone to bear. You're sure Karl wouldn't just turn his back and walk out on that?"

She pursed her lips, her eyes welled, and she shook her head. "I couldn't ever let myself believe he would do that. I just couldn't live with that."

"You were going to say something?" I suggested.

"Yes, about us never getting out from under that debt. That's not true. As of today, we owe less than a million. Karl's salary is four hundred thousand a year, which isn't as much as it sounds, after taxes and garnishment, two college tuitions and four parents in assisted living. But—"

And here again was the brightness.

"—something changed in the past few weeks. Amid all his stress, he was starting to show some optimism. He was looking at houses on Zillow. Nice houses, full of light, in the nicer developments just ten minutes from here. He'd send me the ones he liked, and I'd fantasize about having more space, more light, a swimming pool even!

"He was looking at vacations too. And I'm not talking about a weekend at Ocean City. I mean, he was looking at Paris and Nice and the Caribbean."

"You think he was expecting some kind of bonus?"

"I think so."

"Was it in his contract? A performance incentive?"

"His contract had a vague clause about bonuses to be determined by the CEO."

"By Leighton Graham?"

"That's right. But Leighton can be capricious. He might give you a pile of money, he might give you nothing at all. He's an autocrat. Ask him why he does something, and he'll blow up at you."

"Did your husband have a time frame for buying the houses he was looking at?"

Erica shook her head. "No. But for the vacations, he was thinking early fall."

"This fall? Like two or three months out?"

She nodded.

"Okay. To change topic here for a minute, when was the last time you saw your husband?"

"Sunday, around seven p.m. We had dinner at this table, and then he went out."

"You know where he went?"

"To the office."

"The big building in Reston Town Center?"

"No. The other one, out past Ashburn."

"Ashburn? Where all the big data centers are?"

The highways out there are lined with windowless warehouses containing hundreds of thousands of Amazon and Google servers. If you stream video in the Eastern U.S., that's where it comes from. If you shop online or do a search, the bits go into and out of those fenced-in cream-and-tan behemoths flanked by rows of truck-size diesel generators to keep the machines running when the power goes out.

"Past there," she said. "And it's not one of the big new facilities. It's an older brick building."

"Why would a talent firm have an office out there? Seems kind of out of the way."

"Karl wanted to get the team out of the Reston office because there were too many distractions," she said. "Some of the other managers seemed to think the developer team was available for their pet projects. Leighton didn't object to the move because the rent was cheap. He's ruthless about cost-cutting, even down to the toilet paper."

"Seriously?"

"Seriously. His job is to boost the company's profits and stock price. If he hits his numbers, he gets a bonus. If he doesn't, he just gets his salary, which is a lot, but for a man like Leighton, a lot is never enough."

"Okay, so Karl went out to the office Sunday night around seven."

"He got there at seven thirty-eight."

"How do you know that?"

"Because he called me. And he always shared his location. I could see it on the iPad. He was still there at ten. And then his location disappeared."

"Disappeared?"

"He sometimes put his phone in airplane mode when he was working. I went to sleep at eleven."

We talked a while longer. The last thing I wanted to know was whether there had been any other changes in his behavior recently, any odd behavior.

"Just the optimism," she said. "Looking at houses and vacations. Oh, and he hurt his back."

"When?"

"A few weeks ago. He fell off a ladder while cleaning the gutter."

"Did the doctor give him meds?"

"Percocet."

"That's an opioid," I said.

"Yes, and he was worried about it. After the accident, he was scared of all drugs. He asked me to keep the pills, and I handed them out to him exactly on schedule. He didn't trust himself."

I thought for a second, then asked. "When did he start looking at houses and vacations? Was it around the same time he started taking the pills?"

"I think so, yes. Just in the last few weeks."

"So maybe he was just daydreaming about this bonus, about this money coming in. You know, the opioids can get your mind going, start you fantasizing. You think the pills might have been responsible for his attitude change?"

She shrugged. "I don't know."

4

In the car outside Erica Larsson's house, I checked the responses from Ed and Claire. They had both reviewed the contract and said it was okay.

From Ed: *Go ahead and sign. And why is the rate so high on this one?*

Asshole surcharge, I replied.

Ed: *Gotcha.*

Claire also picked up on the rate change, but she was more interested in the addendum Graham's lawyer had added, the forced end-of-day meetings.

Claire: *I know that type. Saw lots of them in the C-level suites in NYC. I'll tell you about it over dinner.* She signed off with a kiss emoji.

She's a sharp observer and a good judge of character. Spent time in the corporate world doing audits and financial investigations before she came on board with us.

She started with us as a contract-to-hire, did a superb job, and we offered her a position. We had a tense week before she actually signed the offer. As a firm of five, we're pretty close-knit. I'm co-owner, along with Ed, and she's technically an employee. That's an awkward setup when you're dating.

Claire and I called an all-hands meeting and told the team we were seeing each other. She wasn't going to sign on unless everyone was on board.

Ed, a retired FBI agent who had founded the firm before bringing me on as partner, asked a lot of tough questions. What if we didn't get along? What if Claire—who can be pretty damn sure of herself—didn't want to take orders from me? What if I didn't want to take orders from her? What if we were fighting outside of work? Would we bring that into the office? Would we allow our feelings to screw up an investigation?

The answer to every one of those questions was "We'll do our best." That's as much as anyone can promise.

We were there to ask if the team would be okay with this experiment. It might work out, and it might blow up in everyone's faces.

Leon, as expected, had no opinion on the matter. For all his researching skills and technical brilliance, he has zero understanding of social dynamics. He finally got tested this year and was confirmed on the autism spectrum. He started researching autism, because he researches everything, and after reading a few articles that described his outlook and behavior to a tee, he turned to Bethany and said, "Why is there a label for this? It's just normal."

Which, to him, it is.

Bethany, with her pale freckled skin and straight strawberry blond hair, just rolled her eyes, as if explaining it to him was pointless. He wouldn't have cared anyway. He was who he was, and he liked himself that way. In his mind, everyone else had a problem because they let extraneous matters like feelings and public opinion blind them to the rigorous logic that was so obvious to him. Leon could listen to a heated argument, filter out the emotions that clouded everyone else's perception, and calmly tell you who was right. Bethany, meanwhile, would get caught up in the feelings and somehow manage to agree with both sides at once.

She was fascinated by Leon, and protective of him.

When Claire and I told the team we were dating and asked for their blessing in this potentially dangerous personal-professional relationship, I thought we were dropping bombshell news. Bethany let out a sigh of annoyance.

"What?" I asked.

"She knew," Claire said. Knew about us, that is. Our announcement was no surprise to her. Bethany's intuition flicked like a snake's tongue, tuned-in to every vibration in the environment.

"Everybody knew, Freddy. Except you." Bethany threw in another eye roll to emphasize that the whole world knew I had a thing for Claire. But that wasn't true. Leon didn't know. Ed thought I was going crazy, or drinking too much, or just having a general breakdown.

And I did know. I just couldn't express it because it didn't seem right to show that kind of interest in someone I had brought on board and was mentoring. Teachers don't hit on students. Bosses don't hit on employees. Those were two red lines I wasn't willing to cross.

But nature has its way. I learned one evening that on the other side of those two red lines, Claire was working just as hard to hold back the same feelings.

What a night that turned out to be!

So the vote came in. Bethany was fine with us trying it out. She even had a little romantic streak I hadn't known about. She was rooting for us.

Leon didn't care one way or the other.

Ed, Claire, and I were all on the fence. We went into Ed's office and settled it like adults, adding some language to Claire's contract. If things got bad, Ed would mediate. Claire could leave the firm at any time, if she felt things weren't working out. She'd get severance and a guaranteed good recommendation, unless she committed some material breach of duty, which I could never see her doing. The woman is so damn smart and self-assured, not to mention experienced, that she could land a job anywhere.

So, now we were ten months into this experiment, and so far, so good. The only one who had had a problem with it was me. I worried about her sometimes. She'd be out following some cheating husband or digging through some political candidate's garbage, and who knew what she might run into?

I'd been beat up, locked up, and shot in the course of the job, but I never worried about myself. I'm tough. I can fight. Very few people in this world scare me, and I know how to handle myself around the ones who do.

When I lay in bed at night thinking through how I might approach a dangerous confrontation, I thought purely in terms of strategy and tactics—the same way I thought when I was boxing professionally. Minimize your opponent's advantages. Maximize your own.

When I thought of her walking into danger, I couldn't sleep. If someone did something really bad to her, well... I couldn't even go there.

Now, leaving Erica's house, it was already 3:30 p.m., and I wanted to take a look at the building where Karl Larsson worked, his last-known whereabouts.

I called Leighton Graham. He rejected my call after two rings, so I called again. He rejected me again. When I called a third time, he said, "This my cell phone. Call my damn secretary," and hung up.

I should have known to start with her. Her number was in my call history. I tapped it and— "This is Freddy. I was in there two hours ago—"

She remembered.

"I need to know the address of Karl Larsson's office. And I need someone to call ahead and tell them I'm coming. I assume the building is restricted access?"

"You assume correctly," she said. She was brisk and efficient, while maintaining the friendly tone her boss so sorely lacked. I don't know how she put up with him.

She gave me the address and told me I'd have to show ID to get in.

I thanked her and wished her a nice day, and not just because I meant it. I wanted to be on good terms with someone in that office. Otherwise, this investigation would never work.

5

Google maps told me that Karl Larsson's office was well past the Ashburn data centers, past the airport and the strip malls and the big box stores, in a part of Loudon County that hadn't yet become the tangle of highways that had ruined Fairfax County.

Twenty minutes west of Reston, the road got narrower, the trees thickened into forests, and cattle grazed in rolling pastures. It was like going back in time, undoing the "improvements" the real estate developers had inflicted on the land. *Someday*, I thought, *maybe Claire and I will live out here, away from the crowds and noise.*

I'd lived in cities all my life: Philadelphia, New York, DC. What did they offer? A million ways to get in trouble. When I was younger, I was the one getting into trouble. Now I'm pushing forty, older and wiser, and what do I do? Investigate problems. Get wrapped up in other people's troubles.

Erica Larsson impressed me as a good, moral person. Not the type to go looking for messes. But trouble found her anyway, years ago in California. She married a man who made a mistake and she stuck with him and helped him carry the burden of that mistake. And this week, trouble found her again. Or found him.

And now... Now I started thinking Google Maps had to be wrong, because no one would put an office out here among the farms and woods. There weren't even housing developments out here yet.

But lo and behold, after one last turn off the two-lane road onto an even narrower road, I saw a brick building, about twenty feet high, surrounded by an asphalt lot and a dozen cars. I pulled in, parked, and took in the scene. To the rear of the building was a view of a small mountain, an outlier of the Blue Ridge. To the left and right, thick green forest. And behind me, the only road in and out.

I walked around back. The brickwork looked old and uneven, like the building may have settled over the seven or eight decades of its existence. The dual-paned, tinted, high-efficiency thermal windows were new.

A pair of double steel doors in the rear had a shiny new lock. Beside those was a bay door large enough to back a truck up to for loading—one of those steel doors that rolls down from above. This place may have once been a warehouse or a parts depot. The dumpster in front of the loading door told me it wasn't in use anymore.

I circled back to the front. The steel door was locked. To the right was a card scanner for employees to scan in. I peered through the little square window reinforced with crisscross wire, but didn't see anyone. Then I noticed the button. A small rectangular home-style doorbell button. Someone had drilled a hole through the brick to wire it up. I pushed it and—funny thing—I heard the ding-dong of a suburban home doorbell.

When I imagined the engineering center of this billion-dollar company, with its "industry-leading AI providing unparalleled candidate-position matching" (according to their website, anyway), I pictured one of those fancy command centers you see in techno-thriller films. This place—from the outside, anyway—looked more like one of the reclaimed historical buildings you find in the gentrified parts of DC, serving eight-dollar coffees to the Apple laptop crowd.

A woman named Ranya let me in. I guessed she was in her mid-thirties. Brown skin, dark hair and eyes, round cheeks, and a friendly manner. Her accent told me she was from India, or somewhere in that part of the world. I had to show her both my IDs, per instructions from headquarters—driver's license and investigator's license. I wondered if that was because this facility was high-security or if Leighton Graham just liked making things hard for me.

"You're here about Karl?" she asked.

"Yes. Did you work with him?"

"When he was in. Let me show you around."

The main work area was one big open space with multi-monitor desks, high-end ergonomic chairs, and bare brick walls on three sides. One wall in back was lined with black tower computers, workstations with flashing green lights.

The rafters overhead were exposed—thick, dark beams of ancient wood, probably cut from the local forests seventy or eighty years ago. Blue and white wires ran the length of the rafters on either side of the office, leading to Wi-Fi access points with more flashing green lights.

Ranya pointed out the high, narrow windows fifteen feet above the floor. They ran horizontally, six feet long and less than a foot high, too thin for thieves to squeeze through.

"Before we remodeled, those were the only windows."

She explained that the building once held plumbing supplies for a distributor driven out of business by the rise of Lowes and Home Depot and a company called Ferguson.

"That's not you, is it?" She smiled. A joke.

"Not me."

She took me past the fourth wall of the office, the one that wasn't brick. Behind the white drywall lay a hallway and several rooms. A kitchen with two tables that could seat a dozen people. Two bathrooms, intersex, for whoever had to go, and three smaller offices.

"These two," she told me, "are for conferences and whiteboarding."

The first room she indicated had an eight-person oval table and some notes scrawled in green and blue on the whiteboard. The second was smaller, with no table but whiteboards all around, covered with multicolored diagrams.

"Trade secrets," she said with a sly smile. "You don't code, do you?"

"Not in a million years. What's this room?" I pointed to a door across the hall.

"Closet," she said. She opened the door. Inside were cleaning supplies.

"And that?" I pointed back to a door near the front.

"That's going to be security," she said. "Once we finish wiring up the video."

Looking inside, we found four cheap-looking monitors on a fold-out table—the kind you rent for banquets and outdoor tent parties. The monitor cables hung to the floor, attached to nothing.

"We're putting in security cameras," she said. "So Big Brother Graham can keep an eye on us."

Beside the table was a cheap swivel chair, an unplugged electric fan, and an old wooden set of cubbies stuffed with junk leftover from the move: technical books, boxes of sticky notes, keyboards, mice. Someone from Westwood Security had left their uniform jacket on the chair. I didn't imagine they'd be picking that up until October, when the weather started to cool.

Ranya led me out past a dozen coders glued to their monitors in the main work area.

"Who's the guy on the ladder?" I asked.

"He's installing the cameras." She directed my attention to a man sitting at a desk with two monitors. "Mr. Ferguson, this is Tony Nguyen, our lead developer."

Nguyen stood to shake my hand, a polite guy who actually *did* seem pleased to meet me. He was short and slim and pale. I got the sense he didn't spend much time outside. His handshake was weak and limp, which made me think he'd be one of those shy, geeky types who knows how to talk to computers but not to people.

My assumption was wrong. The guy had a confidence and ease I wish I saw more of in this world. He smiled a lot too.

"Ranya gave you the tour?"

"All three minutes of it," I said.

"She tell you what we do here?"

"Not really."

Nguyen's smile lit up, he rolled a chair toward me, and he sat back down and put his arms behind his head like he was winding up for a long tale. Ranya had apparently already heard it. She drifted off to another desk as Nguyen launched into his spiel.

I'll save you twenty minutes of gushing technobabble by boiling it down to this: Recursion used an artificial intelligence engine to sift through reams of data about each candidate and each open position to find the best matches. Then it sent off its ranked list of candidates to the company's recruiters to start the interview process.

"Our recruiters don't waste time interviewing low-value candidates," Nguyen told me. "That puts us ahead of other companies that have more primitive matching systems. It might take them a day or two to find the top three candidates for a job, the ones they should be interviewing. In that time, we've already interviewed them and set up a meeting with the employer."

He told me the company's algorithms feed not just on the resumes the candidates submit, but on publicly available data sucked in from all over the internet.

"The algorithm can tell us a lot about a person just by examining their LinkedIn contacts, their Twitter posts, their Reddit comments."

"Is that legal?" I asked. "I mean, people are looking for a job, they're not granting you permission to dig into their personal lives."

"Actually, according to our end-user agreement, they are."

I've looked at some of those agreements. The ones that say, "by clicking submit, you agree to our terms of service." The terms of service are twenty or thirty pages of legalese that, for all I know, could mean I'm signing over my firstborn.

I let Nguyen go on for a while, not because I was interested in the technology he was talking about, but because *he* was interested in it. Give a person an audience, get them on a roll, and their tongue loosens up. Then, when you get to the important questions, you might get some useful answers because this person actually *likes* talking to you.

"Let's take you, for example," Nguyen said. "Do you mind if I use you?"

"Use me for what?"

"A case study. I'll show you what kind of profile our system can build on you based on your public internet presence."

"I don't have an internet presence."

"Sure you do."

"No, I don't. I'm an investigator. I don't use social media. I don't post photos of myself because then people can identify me. Then they'll know that the guy following them is a detective."

"Huh?" Nguyen seemed genuinely perplexed. "You don't use Facebook?"

I shook my head.

"Instagram? Twitter?"

"No."

He gave me the kind of curious look I might give to a primitive tribesman who had just wandered out of the jungle. "Then how do you keep in touch with people?"

"I talk to them in person."

"Like, at their house?"

"Or the office, or a gym. Or a restaurant. Or a baseball game."

He shook his head. "That's incredibly inefficient. How much do you spend on gas?"

"Never mind. Look, I came here to ask you about Karl Larsson."

"What about Karl?"

"He disappeared."

Nguyen was still giving me that man-out-of-the-jungle look.

"Yeah, I know," he said at last.

"Did Ranya tell you I'm an investigator?"

He shook his head.

Oh, Christ! I showed him my PI license, just so there would be no doubt.

"Ok," I said. "Larsson's last known location was here, in this building, Sunday night."

Nguyen nodded, mouth slightly open, still struggling with the idea of a person who didn't live online.

"Was that normal for him?" I asked. "To be out here on a Sunday night?"

"Um... I wouldn't say it's abnormal. He's the CTO, so he splits his time between the Reston office and here. But he prefers being here. He's more of a techie than an executive type. He's a hands-on guy. He even reviews my code. Like, regularly. Not many CTOs do that. That's why the team likes him so much. He's one of *us* who happened to make it all the way up into the executive suite."

Nguyen repeated what Erica Larsson had told me, that it was Larsson's idea to move the developer team out here.

He pointed to the ranks of computers near the rear wall. "Those are high-end, GPU-optimized workstations," he gloated. "A terabyte of RAM in each one! It's actually cheaper to run some workloads on-prem than in the cloud. Anything compute- or GPU-intensive..."

He trailed off when he saw he'd lost me. Then he started over on a different tack.

"Ok, back at HQ, we had managers from other departments coming in all the time, telling us they wanted this feature and that feature. And Leighton Graham was there too. He's a micro-manager who thinks he owns everyone who works for him. Like, literally owns them."

He told me Larsson knew his team would be more productive if he isolated them from internal politics, conflicting demands, and meddling executives.

"And he was right," Nguyen said. "We're way more productive out here."

I asked him most of the same questions I'd asked Erica. Did Karl have any enemies? Affairs or outside love interests? Nguyen seemed taken aback. "How would I know?"

I didn't expect he would, but I had to ask. For a guy like Larsson, who spent so much time in the office, the most likely candidate for an affair would be a coworker.

Did Larsson fear anyone? Had his behavior changed recently?

"His brain was running a little slower when he was on meds," Nguyen told me. "He hurt his back and whatever painkillers he was taking seemed to dull his mind, but you wouldn't notice unless you knew him. I'd say he was operating at about eighty percent. And Karl at fifty percent would still be smarter than most people at a hundred percent."

"No other behavior changes?" I asked. "No signs of nervousness, furtiveness, agitation, anything like that?"

Nguyen shook his head. "No. He actually seemed a little happier than usual."

"Optimistic?" I asked. I wanted to see if his observation meshed with Erica's.

"Yeah. I guess you could say that."

Nguyen introduced me to a few other team members who had worked closely with Larsson. They all told me the same thing. No unusual behavior. No sign that anything was wrong. Larsson seemed to have a fairly positive mindset.

I asked them if anyone else was in the office Sunday night, the night Larsson disappeared.

"No one," said Ranya. "But I was online. I could see he was signed into Slack and actively working. He had the little green dot next to his name."

"Does anyone else come into this building? A cleaning crew?"

"Cleaners come Monday and Thursday evenings. Security checks the lot every hour or two. They come into the building and do a walk through a couple times a night. I don't know exactly when."

"The security company is called Westwood?" I asked, remembering the jacket in the office up front.

"I think so."

Okay, I thought. *That's something.*

I thanked Ranya for the tour, thanked the others for their time, then went to find Nguyen to tell him I might be back in touch.

He was standing in the rear corner, greedily pulling pages off the laser printer. When I reached him, he turned with a smile and said, "Claire Chastain."

"What?"

"She works for your firm."

"How did you know that?" I asked. We don't list employee names on our website, just our areas of expertise.

"The internet," he said. "Actually, our AI found her. I wanted to give you a sample of what kind of profile we can build. I started with her LinkedIn profile and worked from there."

"She doesn't have a LinkedIn profile," I said. "She took it down over a year ago."

"We crawl the web twenty-four-seven. We got a snapshot of it before it went offline. In fact, we have thirty snapshots of it. We can tell how she edited it over time. And she's a damn good writer."

"You can tell that from LinkedIn?"

"I can tell it from the memos and reports she wrote when she was a contractor at the Securities and Exchange Commission."

"Where did you find those?"

"In court filings. The cases are all public."

"You pull data from court cases?"

"To train our AI. Any public record is fair game. We pull all of it."

He handed me the report, a three-page profile written by a machine.

"Read it!" Nguyen had the eagerness of a kid showing off his new toy.

It was 5:20. Some of the employees were packing up and leaving. I was supposed to be back in Reston at 6:00 to give Graham his daily in-person report. In rush hour traffic, I'd be cutting it close.

"I'll read it later," I said. "I have to get to a meeting."

Outside, a workman was up on his ladder, drilling through the brick to wire up a camera that would monitor the only road leading into and out of this place.

A little late for that, I thought. The cameras should have been in two nights ago, when Karl disappeared.

The drive back to Reston was depressing. Forests and rolling hills and fields of horses gave way to crowded highways, toll booths, 7-11s, exhaust fumes, and impatient commuters.

6

I got to Graham's office ten minutes early and had to wait on the leather sofa in the reception area. The sixty-inch flatscreen mounted on the opposite wall was tuned to the financial news on CNBC.

Thirty minutes later, I was *still* on that couch. Graham had told me to be on time and now he was making me wait. While I was there, the news anchor reported the results of Recursion Talent's quarterly earnings report, which had just been released after the markets closed.

"A stunning turnaround from a year ago," he said, and went on to give some numbers that "far exceeded analysts' expectations." Recursion's stock was up on after-hours trading and was expected to open higher at tomorrow's morning bell.

You'd think with such rosy news, Graham would be in a better mood, but he wasn't. Maybe he didn't hit whatever target the board had set for him, the profit target that would trigger his bonus. Maybe he just wasn't capable of good moods when he had to deal with hired help like me.

When he opened the door—his assistant had already left— he was holding his cell phone to his ear and waved me in with a scowl.

"You said it would be done at six," he barked. "How hard is it to find a fucking headlight and grille? You're a goddamn Mercedes dealership. You can pull the parts off another car."

He paused for a few seconds while the person on the other end tried to get a few words in.

"Look, I don't fucking care, okay? I want my fucking car, A-S-A-fucking-P. Do you get that?"

He ended the call and slid his phone into his pocket as I passed by.

"Why can't people keep their damn dogs in the yard?"

"You hit a dog?"

I could see the contract on the desk waiting for my signature. Part of me wanted to throw in one last change, to bill in six-minute increments, the way lawyers do. I could have pulled in a couple hundred bucks for the forty minutes I spent waiting in reception.

"The dog hit my car," Graham growled.

"He okay?"

"Who cares? Sign that." He meant the contract with his prima donna addendum.

I don't know why I asked about the dog. If the impact was hard enough to damage the headlight and grille of a Mercedes, the dog probably wasn't okay.

I picked up the pen and signed. One copy for him, one for me. I folded my copy and kept it in hand.

I didn't sit because he was standing behind me, hovering in my space, which always makes me uneasy. So I turned to face him, my back to his desk and the giant west-facing windows with the evening sun streaming in. I made him squint at me.

"What'd you learn?" he asked.

I started to give him a summary of my visit with Erica Larsson, but he cut me off and told me he didn't want a summary. He wanted full details.

"You seriously want me to stand here and rehash an hour-long conversation?"

"What does the contract say?"

"It says I give you a full account at the end of every day. It also says either one of us can walk at any time if this isn't working out. I'm not going to spend an hour telling you something I can get across in five minutes, and if you don't want the five-minute version, I'll give you nothing."

He walked around me and stood at the window, positioning himself to the right of the blinding sun. Now I was squinting to see him.

"Alright," he said. "Out with it."

I told him what I'd learned from Larsson's wife. No strange behavior, a mistress was unlikely, but the family had struggled under heavy debt for years.

"That's all she told you?" There was a challenge in his tone, irritated and impatient.

"That's all that's relevant."

"You sure?"

"I'm pretty sure."

"Pretty sure isn't the same thing as sure. What about the Percocet?"

"What about it?" I asked.

"Why didn't you mention that?"

"Because I don't think it's an issue."

"I'll decide what's an issue. Tell me what you learned at the dev center where Karl worked."

"Wait, if the Percocet is an issue and you knew about it, why didn't you tell me about it yourself? Do you think it was affecting his work? Did you talk to Karl about it?"

"I'll run the business, Freddy. You stick to the investigation. What did you learn at Karl's office?"

I'd had enough of his domineering tone. "When I ask questions, I ask them for a reason. Every bit of information gets us closer to an answer. You want to solve this case or not? Because being a fucking prick isn't helping anyone."

I could tell he wasn't used to people talking to him that way, and I could tell he sure as hell didn't like it. The guy reminded me of those dirty fighters I'd run across on my way up the heavyweight division, the ones who hit you in the back of the head during a clinch, who hit your kidneys and break your nose with an "accidental" headbutt.

The psychology of those guys always bugged me. They had to get the best of every exchange. Or I should say, they had to *think* they got the best of every exchange. In the long run, they weren't always the best fighters, and I found the thing that bothered them the most was a good jab.

A jab isn't a particularly hard punch. It's a tactical punch. You use it to keep a guy from setting up and unloading on you. You use it to set up your own power punches. You use it to keep dirty fighters at a distance, so they can't pull you in and land those rabbit punches to the back of your head.

Jabs work in conversation too. You get a guy like Graham, a guy who looks at every encounter as an exchange that has a winner and a loser, a guy determined to always be on top. Guys like that, whether they're boxing or playing their little domination game in the executive suite—you poke them too many times, they start to lose their cool.

I always liked to start with a stiff jab, one that would snap my opponent's head back and wake him up.

That was what I gave Graham. The same short, disrespectful tone he dealt out to others. I wanted to see how much he enjoyed being on the receiving end of it.

He didn't like it at all. His nostrils flared and the color in his cheeks rose. I saw him size me up, like for a second there he seriously considered hitting me. And I saw him decide that wouldn't be a good idea.

I actually respected him a little more for that, for seriously entertaining the idea of hitting me. Some bullies are full of bluster with nothing to back it up. I got the sense Graham didn't mind mixing it up. He'd probably been in a few fights and had probably won some. I don't think he was scared of me. He just decided I'd be more trouble than he felt like dealing with at that moment.

So yeah, my respect for him on a hundred-point scale jumped from zero to one.

And then he went right back to the power game, because it was the only game he knew.

"Tell me about the dev center, Freddy."

Angry, assertive tone, with no acknowledgment of what I'd just said.

Screw it, I thought. *I'm not sinking to his level. One of us is going to be the adult here. Just give him the report and move on.*

"I talked to Ranya and Tony Nguyen and a few other people. Larsson was out there alone on Sunday night. No other employees. There's one road in and one road out. By the way, what's up with the security cameras out there?"

"We're replacing them."

"Was there a working surveillance system the night Karl disappeared?"

"If there had been, we wouldn't need your help."

Now that was a funny thing to say. I mean, I get that this guy likes to be a prick, that he enjoys verbal sparring, that he gets his power trip by abusing other people and appearing to be in charge, but as Leon would put it, his statement was not logically correct.

Say there had been working surveillance cameras out there. What would they show? They'd show Karl driving in, Karl parking. They'd show him in the office, and they'd show him leaving the office. Finally, they'd show his car driving out of the lot, because it wasn't there on Monday morning.

So how would that get us any closer to discovering where he'd gone? Unless something happened right there at the office, an assault or an abduction caught on camera.

I was quiet a little too long, and Graham didn't like it.

"What's on your mind, Freddy?"

"The dev team told me you have a private security company swing by there every couple of hours."

"It's the same team that patrols this building. A private firm."

"I'm going to talk to them tomorrow, find out who was on duty, what time they drove by, whether they did a walkthrough of the office or just drove around the lot."

"And then?"

"We'll see what we learn."

He stared at me for a moment, a judging stare, a sizing-me-up stare, and he made no effort to hide the result of his judgment. He didn't think much of me. I was a low-level grunt stuck in a life of pounding the pavement for people like him, and the reason I was stuck there was because I wasn't as smart as him, or as driven, or as ambitious. People like me set ourselves up to be used by people like him. That was the order of the world as he saw it, and it was a natural, inviolable order.

"This is how you operate?" he said. "You go blindly poking around like a dog sniffing in the woods, hoping to stumble onto something?"

He was baiting me with that contemptuous tone. He had already got me to snap at him once, and now he wanted to see how far he had to push me before I'd lose my cool. I wasn't going to bite on that. It was just another power play, like guys testing each other in the ring. Or in prison.

"I like to think I'm a little more organized than that," I said calmly. "Running an investigation isn't like running a business. A business has a lot of *knowns*. You know who your customers are. You know how much it costs to build your product. You can make plans because you know what you're working with.

"An investigation starts with an unknown. What happened? Not much is given. You have to go out and track down the facts, build up the knowns one by one, follow from one lead to the next. The truth is out there. It leaves its traces everywhere, but you won't find them unless you look.

"If Larsson had any reason to run away," I said, "it would be debt. I believe his wife, that he wouldn't run out on her, but I've heard equally convincing tales of devotion from other spouses whose partners really did run off. And I've also seen cases that were completely random. A guy's in the wrong place at the wrong time, gets robbed or carjacked coming out of a gas station. His disappearance had nothing at all to do with the way he was living.

"Let me ask you something. You knew about Larsson's accident because you worked with him in California. You knew he'd used cocaine then, and you're worried about him using Percocet now. You think the guy had drug problems?"

Graham slid his hands into his pockets and strolled away from the window toward a wall hung with modern paintings. He stopped by one that looked like a giant, blown-up panel from a comic book.

"I really couldn't say."

"You knew the guy was struggling financially. Why didn't you help him out?"

"I did help him out. I'm the one who brought him on here."

"I know, but the guy was really in a hole. Maybe I don't fully get how big business works, but it seems you C-level executives are pretty generous in giving each other bonuses."

"I came here to cut costs," Graham said angrily. "To turn this operation around, not to hand out cash to pity cases."

Pity cases? After the conversation I had with Erica Larsson, I had thought there was at least a working level of respect between Graham and his CTO. From what I'd seen of him so far, Graham wouldn't hire anyone out of pity. Larsson had to be an effective worker. Where's the pity case here?

I wanted to throw one last thing at Graham, just to see how he'd react.

"I saw the news," I told him. "When you left me out there waiting, CNBC said your quarterly earnings beat expectations. Does that mean you got your bonus?"

His grin told me it did. It was a wolfish grin, more malignant and self-satisfied than happy. The corporate axe man had been rewarded by the board for the butchering he'd inflicted on this company.

7

It was past 7:00 when I left. I was supposed to be having dinner with Claire, but such is the life of an investigator. You make plans, and then you end up working late, and you hope your partner can roll with it. She's pretty good about that. I had texted her from Graham's office, when he'd kept me waiting out on the couch. Claire said she'd pick up Indian food, and I could warm it up when I got back.

One thing was still bothering me as I left the Town Center complex. Erica Larsson's house wasn't too far away, so I figured I'd swing by and ask before making the long haul back to DC.

When I arrived on her street, someone must have been having a party, because every parking spot was taken. It was the house two doors down from hers, with barbecue smoke rising from the backyard and the sound of shrieking kids and parents loosening up with beer and wine.

I drove to the end of the block and parked around the corner. The guy behind me in the blue Ford Explorer was in the same boat, hunting for a spot. He drifted past and I watched the old chugger with its dented rear end pull into a space down the street.

I walked back to Larsson's house and rang the bell. She answered a minute later, wearing the same blue skirt and scoop-neck shirt she'd worn earlier, only now her feet were bare and her eyes were sad, and she smelled like cheap wine.

"Hello, Freddy."

I got the sense she was sinking into quicksand. After all the years of hardship and holding out hope, her husband gets this spark of optimism and starts talking like things are going to change, and then all of a sudden—bam! He disappears. It's the blows you don't see coming that really floor you.

"You want to come in?"

"No, thanks though." I could see clear through to the kitchen behind her, the black box on the counter beside the sink. She was drinking wine from a box, alone.

"I wanted to ask you something," I said. "A couple things, actually. First off, why would Karl want to work with a guy like Graham?"

"Because Graham offered him a position. A good one."

"But with Karl's skill and experience, couldn't he have landed a similar job at another company?"

I don't know if it was the wine or the fact that she had never really explored the question on her own, but she didn't have an answer for that.

"I don't know," was all she could muster.

"Because Graham's not a pleasant guy. I can't imagine having to answer to someone like him day in and day out."

"You do what you have to do," she said. "When times are bad."

"Ok, second question. You said Karl had been acting like the money situation was going to turn around soon. Graham had a big bonus coming if the company hit its earnings target. Do you know if Karl had a similar clause? Was he expecting a bonus?"

"Oh, no," she said. I could see the effect of the wine in the sloppy shake of her head. "The company was a mess. It's been in the news for months. There was no way they were going to hit their numbers."

"But they did," I said.

"No." She shook her head again. "It was all going down the tubes. You can look it up on Bloomberg or MarketWatch or any of those sites."

"But—" I stopped myself. She hadn't seen the news. She hadn't been tuned-in to CNBC that evening, and she wasn't tuned-in to anything at the moment. She was tuning out, in fact, and maybe that's what she needed.

I thanked her and wished her a good evening.

When I drove off, the blue Explorer was still idling at the end of the block. The guy in the driver seat had his face in his phone.

At least turn off the engine, I thought. These stupid phones are making us all brain-dead. You see those dystopian horror shows about the zombie apocalypse— Well we're already there. Only it wasn't some virus or toxin that rotted out our brains. It was the iPhone and the Android.

8

I was going to stop by my place, shower and change before
going over to Claire's. Graham's ill-tempered arrogance stuck
to me like grime. I wanted to wash it off and meet her fresh,
but she called as I was crossing the Beltway and said to come
straight over.

We spend more time in her apartment than mine. She thinks
my apartment is gross. I have to say, I disagree. My apartment
has everything I need, and everything is in exactly the right
place. If it's dirty, I clean it. The problem is, we have different
definitions of "dirty."

If dust accumulates on a shelf I don't use, then someday
when I have nothing better to do, I'll clean it. Her shelves don't
have dust. I tried doing to them what she did to my shelves,
writing "Clean me" with my finger, but nothing showed up.
That kind of pissed me off, because every shelf in my
apartment said "Clean me," and I don't like graffiti, so I had to
spend an hour dusting the place.

Then there's the bed issue. After the second night she spent
at my place, she said, "How often do you change these sheets?"

I said, "Are they stained?"

"No."

"Then why do I have to change them?"

"Ok," she said, "there's my answer right there."

So I bought five sets of sheets, all different colors, and I change them every time she stays over. And she *knows* I change them, because last time they were blue and this time they're yellow.

Did she notice this thoughtful act of mine? She did. And what did she say about it? She said none of the colors I picked matched the decor. Did I think about that when I bought them?

Not at all. My apartment doesn't even have a decor. It just has stuff. *My* stuff. The point of the colored sheets was to let her know they'd been changed and she could stop worrying about cooties, or whatever the hell she thought might be lurking in there. That part worked, but having to wash the bedding all the time sucked because they took up the whole machine and they got twisted in the dryer and came out damp.

Her place… Well you can tell she put some thought into it. The furniture and the artwork and the rugs all match. Even the dishes. She happens to like light blues and greens. Her apartment gets good sunlight, and the colors keep the mood bright.

Her place is spare, mine is cluttered. Sometimes I think our living spaces are external manifestations of our minds. A million things run through my mind in a day, in no particular order, and there's room for all of them. She's more to the point. You read her reports, there's no junk in there. No wasted words, no clutter. She puts all her thoughts in order before they hit the page.

When I got to her place near Woodley Park, I told her I needed a shower.

"Let's eat first," she said.

It was eight o'clock, and she had waited for me. The boxes of Indian food were unopened and still warm, which told me she had just picked them up.

Another thing, she was wearing her red pajamas. The thin cotton ones, the ones that always make me want her.

But I wasn't there yet. I was still grouchy from having to deal with Graham, and I knew from being married to Miriam not to bring my bad mood to dinner.

We ate at the kitchen table. Claire doesn't eat much meat. I do. She loaded up with curried prawns and spinach saag while I went for the tandoori chicken.

"I looked into that company you're working for." Her smile and the light in her eyes told me she'd had a good day. It doesn't take much more than that to make me feel better.

"Yeah?"

"Leighton Graham has a reputation as a turnaround artist."

"Artist is not the word I'd use to describe that man."

She laughed. "Did you see they published their earnings report today? Seems he turned things around."

"So he did."

"That was a surprise," she said. "Oh, and..." She got up, went the fridge, and returned with a bottle of white wine, already open and not quite full.

"I see you already had a glass," I said.

"It's good." She poured for both of us, then sat and said, "Those earnings were a big surprise."

She followed this kind of news. She had worked in New York for years, evaluating companies' finances and internal health on behalf of bigger companies that wanted to buy them out.

"The funny thing," she said, "is that if you'd been reading the news the past few months, it sounded like they were circling the drain. The industry wisdom said Graham had cut too deep. Morale was in the tank and the company didn't have enough remaining staff left to pull off this kind of turnaround."

"I can't imagine working for that guy."

I added rice and spinach to my plate.

"You want my prediction?" she asked.

"Shoot," I said. I liked her predictions. They were usually right.

"Nazari Khan is going to get fired."

"Who is Nazari Khan?" I asked through a mouthful of rice.

"A Wall Street reporter whose coverage is usually spot on. He's the one who's been sounding the death knell for Recursion Talent these past few months. The guy has never been this wrong before. In fact, I don't think he's ever been wrong at all."

She gave me the lowdown. In the kind of slash-and-burn restructuring that Graham had been implementing, it was normal for a company to lose money for several quarters. They had to pay out severance, and the reduced staff had to adjust to a heavier workload. Morale inside the company and doubts among the clients could hurt revenues.

"If the company didn't turn around this quarter," Claire said, "it might have gone into a death spiral. That's the scenario Nazari Khan was describing. He had inside information. He always has inside information, because he's cultivated a huge network of sources. And he's always right. He's been reporting for months that the company was on its deathbed. All the other reporters started repeating him and it killed the company's stock price. Now Leighton Graham has the last laugh. I bet he's pleased with himself."

"And you think they'll fire this reporter?"

"I would. It's okay to be wrong sometimes, but you can't be *that* wrong and still maintain credibility. Especially in finance. How's that spinach?"

"Excellent."

Then it was my turn to get up. I wanted to show her that report Tony Nguyen had printed out for me, the assessment his artificial intelligence program had made of Claire. I'd read it through twice while waiting on the black sofa outside Graham's office.

I handed it to her and watched her read. I like the look of intense focus she gets when her mind is engaged. The little crease that appeared in her brow after a minute told me she had taken issue with something in the report. I wasn't sure what. I thought the assessment was dead on.

The AI program understood her areas of expertise: business, finance, accounting, and much of the law surrounding those fields. That was easy enough for a computer to glean, given that it had read her résumé and a number of memos she'd written while working as a contractor at the Securities and Exchange Commission.

The computer also figured out that she's detail oriented and an exceptionally clear thinker. Again, you could infer that from her writing.

What got me though was this:

She works well as part of a team, and will encourage others to match her high standards, but only if she has decision-making authority. If not challenged, she will become bored and seek challenges elsewhere.

That's her all right, and when I read it, my first thought was there's no way a computer could have written that. Tony Nguyen must have slipped it in while I was interviewing other members of Larsson's team.

But how could *he* have known? He had never met Claire. It really was the computer that had figured that out.

"How does it know all this?" Claire asked, setting the report down on the table. "What information was it trained on?"

"A copy of your old LinkedIn profile," I said. "One it had saved before you deleted it. And some things you wrote for the SEC that are publicly available."

"It read more than that," she said. "I wonder where it found it all."

We talked for a few minutes about how the new artificial intelligence engines might change the world. Stable Diffusion could generate realistic photos and paintings from a brief description. ChatGPT could write whole articles about anyone and anything you asked for.

"Where does this end?" Claire asked. "How will anyone on the internet know what's real and what's been made up by a machine?"

I told her that soon we'd have AI bots committing crimes and other AI bots solving them, and the only thing left for humans to do would be to grow food and make love.

Claire put her fork down, walked around behind me, and started rubbing my shoulders.

"You're tense."

She leaned in and kissed my neck. "Wanna loosen up?"

Those pajamas and the scent of her skin got me wound up. I told her I needed to shower first.

"Go for it."

From the hard-edged personality she presented to the world, I would not have guessed this woman would be so affectionate. But I've been surprised before. My ex-wife, Miriam, was the incarnation of warmth and tenderness when we were dating. After we tied the knot, she was hot-tempered and combative.

I'm not saying it was a character flaw. She's not that way with her current husband, so I have to assume it was something in the dynamic between us. Claire and I had been dating for six months when it hit me one day in the shower, when I was finally able to put into words the difference between this relationship and the marriage that fell apart.

With Miriam and me, if one of us was in a bad mood, we'd drag the other one down. With Claire and me, if one of us was in a good mood, we lifted the other one up.

On any given day, between any two people, there's a damn good chance that one is in a better mood than the other. With Miriam, we always sank. With Claire, we always rose. And it wasn't through any conscious effort. It just happened naturally.

The shower that night was just the thing to unwind me. I walked out wearing just a towel and found Claire on the bed reading a magazine, still in her red pajamas.

I slid up beside her, kissed her cheek, and said, "Thanks for keeping those on. You know I like to take them off myself."

"You know I like you taking them off."

At 9:30, when it was dark, she lay with her head on my chest.

"I'm going to Indianapolis in the morning," she said.

"New case?"

"Came in today. A man thinks his wife is cheating. She used to hate going to these marketing conferences. Now she goes all the time. Packs nice clothes, leaves in a good mood, comes back kind of distant and wistful. She's doing back-to-back conferences in Indianapolis and Chicago. I registered for both, so I can keep an eye on her."

"Let me guess," I said. "You already checked the conference registrations and made a list of all the guys who will be at both."

"Check!"

"How many names do you have?"

"Seventeen. But who's to say she's seeing just one guy? She could have a lover at every event. Or they could be one-night stands. Or she could be innocent."

"Who's the client?"

"A lawyer in Bethesda."

"What's your sense on this one?"

"I think they hate each other. I think he wants her to be cheating so he can divorce her without it costing half his fortune."

"What gives you that idea?"

"His tone and his overall vibe. He has no love for his wife and he's ready to move on. I saw an envelope on the desk from an attorney who specializes in family law. That tells me he's building a case. The worst thing though was he kept looking at my boobs. And I swear, he twice came within an inch of making a pass at me. I could see it in his eyes."

"What would you have done if he had?"

I already knew the answer to that, but I liked to hear her say it. Claire is an attractive woman—dark hair, dark eyes, fit and strong, with a lively mind and a sometimes-fiery temper—but she's not all that approachable. In public, her presence and manner are always professional. As in, respect me and I will respect you, and let's get down to brass tacks. God help the man who makes a pass at her when there's business to attend to.

"I would have told his wife," she said. "And cost him a fortune."

"So now you're working for someone you don't like."

"Same as you," she said with a yawn.

I knew she'd be asleep in a minute or two. I like to stay awake for a while after she dozes off, especially when her head is on my chest. I like the feeling of her hair on my skin. I like to listen to her breathe.

I wonder sometimes why she granted me an exemption. Why don't I get the same hard edge she presents to the rest of the world? She told me once she trusted me completely, and I've never understood why. Not because I'm not trustworthy. I am. I make it a point to live up to my word, always.

But why does she extend that faith to me that she won't extend to anyone else?

That night, I dreamed she went to the conference and didn't come back. She called and told me in her professional way that the man she'd met in Indianapolis was just too compelling. Her soul was on fire, and thank you, Freddy, for being good to me when we were together, and thank you for teaching me to trust again.

She was gone when I awoke. She was on a plane to the Midwest. And the note she'd left on the nightstand saying she loved me and we'd go out when she got back, that went into my pocket. A good luck charm, a talisman of hope, a counterbalance to that nightmare about losing someone I'd never thought I'd find in the first place.

9

I went back to my place, ate breakfast, and changed. Then I paid a visit to the Fairfax County police. I wanted to know what they'd learned about Larsson's disappearance and how hard they were pursuing it.

My contact there was Jim Burkheim, an older guy nearing the end of his career. He was a good investigator before he burned out. It wasn't the job so much as the drinking. I've seen the guy put down almost a case of beer on a Sunday afternoon watching football. Maybe the job drove him to it. Or maybe his wife did. Or maybe it was his wife walking out on him. Or maybe he just liked to drink.

He didn't do it on the job, but he drank enough after hours to blow up like a balloon. Now they had him behind a desk, riding out his last four months of service. They let him stay on as a favor, so he could leave with a full retirement package, but they made sure to put him in a place where he could do no harm.

Burkheim was in the Reston station, not far from Leighton Graham's office. He had a hand in this case, mainly reviewing reports from other cops. A few years ago, when he was slimmer and less hungover, he might have been leading the investigation.

I found him at a desk in a windowless room at the rear of the building that I swear was a converted janitor's closet. He didn't notice me standing in the open doorway. He was watching cat videos on TikTok.

I rapped my knuckles against the doorpost and said, "Hey, Jim."

"Freddy!" His face lit up. He pushed himself away from the desk with some effort and stood to shake my hand. He was fatter than ever and had big dark bags under his eyes.

It was sad. I wondered how long this guy would make it in retirement, when he no longer had to show up sober anywhere.

"How've you been?"

He always did show a genuine interest in people. I'll give him that.

"Busy," I said.

"Better busy than idle. Means you're getting paid. How's Claire?"

"Claire's great. She's out chasing the wife of a suspicious husband."

"God, I don't know how you guys deal with that crap. Domestic cases are the worst. What are you doing out here?"

I told him I was looking for Karl Larsson.

"Yeah, so are we."

His careless, laissez-faire tone told me all I needed to know about how hard the county was pursuing the case. Missing persons reports come in all the time. Some people call because their partner or their kid was supposed to be home an hour ago.

When there's media pressure, like a little girl gone missing, the department has to be on its toes. In most cases, though, they go out and talk to the same people I'd been talking to: the spouse, the coworkers, whoever had last seen the subject. They make the rounds of the guy's usual haunts: a coffee shop, a gym, a bar. They'll try to find out who he had been communicating with and talk to those people.

They can't put out a dragnet for everyone who doesn't come home on time, and when the leads peter out, there's not much more they can do except keep their eyes open. The county has patrol cars on the streets. They know they're looking for a twelve-year-old, dark blue Mazda CX-7. They know the license plate number.

Jim told me all this, which was what I'd expected. They didn't have any more to go on than I did. If this were a murder case or a high-profile robbery, he wouldn't have told me anything at all, even if he knew exactly what happened and who did it. Cops can't compromise an investigation like that.

But on a case like this—which, to be honest, was a time-consuming pain in the ass for a busy county like Fairfax—the department was perfectly happy to get a helping hand from a private investigator.

Burkheim, sitting in the chair behind his desk, leaned back and put his hands behind his head. "We did get ahold of his call logs from T-Mobile. His chats too."

"Anything there?"

Jim shook his head. "In the past month, he's talked to his wife, his boss, some coworkers, his sons who are attending college out of state, and his parents, who are both in a home in California."

"What about his texts?" I asked. "Any indication of an affair?"

Again he shook his head. "Not on the built-in messaging app, anyway. We talked to Apple and found out what other apps were on his phone. He had Signal. You know what that is?"

"Encrypted chat?"

"With disappearing messages. So whoever he was talking to on that, and whatever he was saying, it's all beyond recovery."

Burkheim had strong opinions about apps like Signal. He felt they shouldn't be allowed to exist. They let terrorists and crime bosses communicate beyond the reach of law enforcement.

"They also let journalists and dissidents communicate in oppressive regimes without being spied on and murdered," I said.

"Yeah, but the United States is not an oppressive regime."

"Depends who you ask," I said. "But keep in mind also that Larsson was a tech guy, and he was high up in the company. A chief technical officer at a large publicly traded company is going to be security conscious."

Claire had told me a few horror stories of executives spilling secrets through texts and unsecured emails. A couple of those cases resulted in shareholder lawsuits and rich guys losing precious millions. Secure communications were a must once you got high enough up the corporate ladder. I was trying to give Larsson the benefit of the doubt here.

"Anything else?" I asked. "Any sign of fear or worry or impending goodbyes in the texts you saw?"

Jim threw up his hands and frowned. "Nothing," he said. "Sorry."

"Well I had to check. The guy I'm working for is a... what's the polite word here? Micro manager?"

"Yeah, we call them assholes."

"I have to be able to tell him I checked in with you guys. So that's one thing I can check off my list."

After talking to Jim, I put in a call to Westwood Security and asked who'd been working the Sunday night shift out at Karl Larsson's office. They wouldn't tell me, so I had to get Graham's assistant to call and explain that the company had hired me and they should answer my questions.

The second time I talked to them, we made some progress. The guy I was looking for was named Lester Tate. He was scheduled to work at 8:00 that evening, which meant he was probably sleeping. I called, and the woman who answered said if I wanted to speak with him, I should try back around 4:00.

That gave me four hours to burn.

I had lunch, then called Erica Larsson and asked if she had access to her husband's computer.

"Not his work computer. He took that with him when he went to the office on Sunday night. But he has a desktop at home."

She was a step ahead of me. She had already logged in to his personal email account and had been combing through his messages.

"How'd you get his password?" I asked.

"We share passwords on LastPass."

Okay. There's a lot of trust in that relationship.

"You find anything?"

"Nothing," she said. "It's all Amazon order confirmations, spam, and messages from me and the kids."

I called Graham's assistant and asked her who would have access to Larsson's company email. She put me in touch with a system administrator.

"I can't give you access to his company email," he said. "We're going through it internally. I can you tell that, so far, we've found nothing of interest, and we've gone back nine months. I don't know if it's even worth going further back."

"How do you know what's of interest and what's not?" I asked. "A lot of times, an innocuous-looking message has a clue, a lead you should follow up on. If you're not an investigator—"

"Mr. Ferguson, we cannot give you access to Karl Larsson's corporate communications. If we find something of interest, we can bring you in to view a redacted copy of the message."

"But this is what I'm saying. Do you even know how to identify *something of interest?*"

"Mr. Ferguson, I cannot give you access to corporate communications." The guy was a broken record. "If I find something and can clear it with legal, I'll let you know."

He hung up.

What was the point of this investigation? Why hire me if you're going to tie my hands?

It was 2:00 in the afternoon and my mood was going south. I was at a dead end and couldn't make another move till 4:00, when Lester Tate would be awake and getting ready for his night shift.

What to do with the next two hours?

I did what I'd found myself doing more and more lately. I drove to a jewelry store and looked at engagement rings.

10

My navigation app led me to a small cinderblock house behind a strip mall in Annandale. A red plastic slide and a pile of toddler toys littered the yard behind a low chain-link fence.

The woman who answered the door held a small child in one arm, and another in her swollen belly. Three more peered out from the room behind her. They couldn't all be hers because they were all about three years old, one white, one black, and one Latino.

I got the picture. Unlicensed neighborhood daycare. She was watching neighbors' kids, kids of parents who barely earned a living wage.

"I help you?" She gave me a suspicious up and down look. I couldn't blame her. A white man showing up unexpectedly at a black woman's door usually wasn't a good sign.

"Is Lester here?"

"Who's asking?"

"Freddy Ferguson." I showed her my investigator's license. "It's not about him. I just want to ask about something he might have seen on the job."

"That white man who disappeared?" She didn't wait for my response. She turned and hollered, "Hey, Lester! Get up here and talk to this man!" The kid in her arm clapped his hands over his ears, too late to shut out the loudness of her voice.

Lester appeared a few seconds later with a slice of toast in his mouth, his Westwood Security shirt unbuttoned to show a clean white tee beneath. He wiped the grease from his hand onto his slacks—his uniform slacks—and shook my hand.

"You the P.I.?"

"Yeah. You have a few minutes?"

"I got a few minutes, but I ain't got nothing to tell you. Cops already been here. I'll tell you the same thing I told them—"

The wail of a child interrupted him. He turned and snapped, "Hey, Lonnie, get that boy. I'm trying to talk here."

"You get that boy!" the pregnant woman snapped. "Or go talk outside."

"I can't deal with this noise!" Lester complained.

"Well why you gonna put it on me then? What do you think I listen to all day?" Then, in a sweeter voice, she cooed to a brown-haired youngster, "Come here, Julio! You want some juice?" She took him by the hand and led him away, shooting Lester the evil eye before disappearing.

"She's all right," he told me. "Just don't get no break, that's all."

No, I thought. Trying to get by on a security guard's salary and whatever the neighbors can spare for childcare, there's no break in that.

Now two kids were screaming.

"Can we talk outside?" I said.

Lester looked back toward where Lonnie had disappeared.

"Better stay here," he said. "Case she needs me. What do you wanna know?"

I asked him what he'd seen last Sunday night when he was doing his rounds. He told me he'd swung by around 10:00 p.m. Larsson's car, the Mazda, was the only one in the lot.

"Did you go in?"

"For a couple minutes. Place was mostly dark, a few desks lit up. Larsson was working on the computer."

"Out in the big, open space?"

"Yeah."

"Then what?"

"Drove a loop around the lot, drove back to Town Center, did a walk-through of the halls, prowled the parking garages."

"Is anyone out that late on a Sunday night?"

"At Town Center? You got hospital staff going in and out of the garages. Ain't really my beat, but I swing by there and check in with their guards. They had a couple nurses get assaulted walking to their cars late at night, so I go by and lend a hand now and then. More security presence means less people hanging around."

Something smashed in the kitchen. Lonnie cursed and a child started to wail.

"Lester!"

"Hold on," Lester said.

I waited almost ten minutes while he helped Lonnie get the situation under control.

When he returned, I asked him to continue. He had forgotten where he'd left off, so I reminded him.

"Yeah, right. Swing by the hospital lot. Then I got some food."

"Where?"

"Seven-Eleven. Couple of hot dogs. Ain't much open that time of night."

Four kids were now tearing through the living room behind Lester Tate. He yelled back into the house, "Lonnie! Come on now!"

"You want to shut the door?" I asked. "Talk in the yard? It's quieter."

"Naw, I'm good."

He ran through the rest of the shift. Another pass through the halls at Recursion's headquarters, a stop in the security office on the ground floor, then swing past six other buildings along the Dulles Access Road.

"When did you get back to Larsson's office? You were supposed to swing by there every few hours, right?"

Lonnie was now chasing one child while carrying another. She was cursing a blue streak. The whole scene made me tense.

A woman that pregnant should not be under that kind of stress.

"Yo, watch the mouth!" Lester said. "Kids gonna take them words home to their parents." Then to me, "What were you asking?"

"What time you got back to Larsson's building for your next check."

"Didn't get back there till the end of my shift, around five a.m."

"What took you so long?"

"Damn!" He laughed. "You're just like the cops, jumping down my throat for being late! I got a call about another building. Supposedly the alarm went off, but there was no alarm when I got there. Spent an hour and a half making sure no one was in the place. You can ask dispatch if you don't believe me."

I made a mental note to check with his dispatcher.

"Was Larsson's car in the lot when you got back for your second check?"

Tate shook his head. "Lot was empty."

"Did you go into the building?"

"Not that time. I looped the lot, went back to headquarters, and clocked out."

"Damn. It would have helped if you'd gone in."

"If I knew the guy was gonna disappear, I would have gone in. Hindsight is twenty-twenty, right?"

"Yeah."

Once again, I had hit a wall. Lester Tate may have been the last person to see Karl Larsson before he disappeared, but Tate had nothing to give me. All I had learned was Larsson's car was in the lot at 10:00 p.m. and gone by 5:00 a.m.

I asked one last question before I left. I think it came from desperation.

"Is there anything else you can tell me about that night?"

"Naw," he said. "I ain't got nothing more to say about that."

But the flash of nervousness, the first he'd shown in our long conversation, and the way his eyes looked away from me told me otherwise.

He turned and went into the house, leaving the door wide open in the August heat. I could hear him and Lonnie and the children yelling as I exited the chain-link gate.

The end of the conversation left me feeling uneasy. That and the blue Ford Explorer with the dent in the back. The same one I'd seen near Erica Larsson's house the night before. I passed it as I left the neighborhood.

It was parked between a red Honda Civic and a white van, so I couldn't see the license plates. I circled the block, hoping to get a look at the driver as I came around, but when I got back, the space between the Honda and the van was empty.

11

I arrived at Leighton Graham's office ten minutes late, just to see if my tardiness would piss him off.

His assistant had left for the day, and the door between his office and the reception area was wide open. Graham was leaning back in his chair with his feet up on the desk, smoking a long cigar. On the desk beside his computer monitor sat a crystal decanter filled with golden-brown liquor.

"Want a drink?" he asked. He actually sounded relaxed for once.

"No thanks," I said. "They let you smoke in here?"

He puffed a billowing blue-grey cloud into the golden sunlight that streamed in through the window behind him.

"You ask the wrong question," he said, and then took another puff. "The question is, who's going to stop me?"

Then he gave me a lecture about how little people and big people have different ways of looking at the world. I had a feeling he'd given this speech before.

"Little people ask what they're *allowed* to do—"

He was interrupted by a chubby young guy in a Westwood Security uniform tapping on the doorpost to get our attention.

"Sir?" said the guard in an uncertain tone. "You can't smoke in here."

"Fuck off," said Graham. "And shut that door."

"Sir? I can smell it out in the hall. I have to report this. Please put that out."

"Report this to whom?" Graham asked. He took his feet off the desk and leaned forward, like he was eager to mix it up with his uncertain, unconfident opponent. "The building owner? Which one of us do you think they care about more? The one who pays a quarter million a month in rent, or the fat incel rent-a-cop who lives in his mom's basement? Get out of here."

The guard looked at me like he wanted help. I made a gesture, zipping my lips, and pointed back out the door, indicating he should leave. Fighting with a guy like Graham is pointless. He only picks battles he can win.

The guard blinked at me, unsure what to do, then he gave up and did as I suggested.

"The kind of people who ask what they're allowed to do," Graham resumed, "go nowhere in life. They become security guards, or they wind up chasing missing people no one cares about because that's the only thing anyone will pay them to do."

I don't know what went wrong in this man's character that made him have to antagonize everyone. I remembered Erica Larsson's words. *A normal person would feel remorse for cutting off the livelihood of thousands of families, but Leighton only sees the bottom line. He's incapable of remorse, and most other human emotions as well.*

And I remembered an article Claire had shared with me a few months ago. Research had shown that the highest concentration of sociopaths in the US were in prisons and CEO suites. It is easier to make tough decisions when you have no empathy for the lives those decisions affect.

But Graham did have some feeling. He wanted people to fear him, and if he couldn't pull that off, then he wanted them to hate him. His task was to get inside you. If you hated him, he owned you. He owned your feelings and drained off the emotional energy you could be putting to better use elsewhere.

Claire told me she had dealt with guys like this on Wall Street. Not many, but enough to develop a strategy to thwart them. She called it "grey rocking."

"You show them no emotion at all," she told me. "Your face is just a blank, grey rock. When they see their manipulation has no effect, it drives them mad. Some of them start to lose confidence. Some just push harder."

I wasn't going to react to Graham's provocations. I took a deep breath and let it out nice and slow and tried to remember the last time I beat the crap out of someone just for the sake of watching them suffer. I think it was back in New York. I think it was that Mafia enforcer I used to pal around with, that giant thug who got off on terrorizing the poor. I hurt him pretty bad, and I got punished for it.

"People who think big go far," Graham said, tipping his ash onto the carpet. He was up out of his seat now, pacing by the window. A one-man show with a captive audience.

"We take what we want because the meek let us take it. You ever notice that, Freddy?" He looked at me then. Not because he really wanted my response. He just wanted to make sure I was paying attention.

He pointed to the traffic crawling along the highway below, the hordes heading home from work. Their cars looked like toys from up here.

"You ever think about how many people there are down below and how few there are up top? You ever think how easy it would be for them to turn the tables? I mean, a million of them against a dozen of us? It would be over in a second. But they don't do it. They never rise up. And you know why? It's because they're weak, and they're meek, and they're unimaginative. Their minds aren't big enough to conceive of changing the world order. And it *is* the world order. Look around you and tell me I'm wrong."

"I'm not going to argue with you, Graham. There are a lot of people worse off than you."

"It's a choice, Freddy." He circled back to the desk, picked up his glass of liquor, and took a sip. "You see the way the world works. Screw or be screwed. I knew when I was four years old which side of that equation I was going to be on, and for all those who choose to be on the other side, well…" He put the glass back on the desk. "They got what they asked for, and I can't say I have much sympathy."

"Thanks for the TED talk, Leighton. You want my report?"

"You know how much they paid me for turning this company around?"

"Jesus Christ, Leighton, I don't fucking care!"

"Six million dollars!"

"Good for you."

"*That* was my bonus!" He slammed his hand on the desk. "Six fucking million! You know how much the CEO of FedEx makes?"

Oh boy, here we go! Leighton's going to have a tantrum because the kid down the street got a bigger toy for Christmas.

For the next couple of minutes he thundered on about the CEOs getting bonuses of twenty and thirty and fifty million dollars, and they didn't turn *anything* around! All they did was helm a ship that was headed in the right direction all along, that could have steered itself and made it into port just fine. Those assholes didn't have the balls to do what he had done here.

He was still ramping up when I cut him off. "You want my report or not? I didn't come out here to waste time."

He had that look again like he wanted to punch me, and then right after it, that look like he better not.

"All right, Freddy." His tone was meant to convey calm, but it sounded more like an angry man trying to show he wasn't ruffled. "Why don't you fill me in?"

I told him about my conversation with Jim Burkheim at the police station, as well as my talk with Lester Tate. He didn't listen to any of it. Didn't even pretend to.

When I finished, he said, "That all you got?"

"That's all."

"All right, get out of here," he snapped. "Come back when you've found Karl."

Grey rocking was harder than Claire made it out to be. Every part of me wanted to wring this guy's neck. I was thinking about him when he wasn't there, on the elevator ride down to the garage, when I should have turned my mind to more fruitful thoughts.

It bugs me that people like him even exist. It bugs me more when they succeed. And succeed they do. What he said about the world order was partially right. Few people rose as high as he had in life, but it wasn't weakness that kept the rest down. Normal people looked out for others, even when it might cost them an opportunity.

But Graham was blind to that. In his view, there was only strength and weakness. He was in love with one and terrified of the other, and everything in his world told him that in choosing strength and contempt, he had made the right choice. The executive suite, the money, the first-class travel, and the AMG Mercedes with its vanity plates parked in the specially marked, reserved space underground. They all confirmed he was right.

I stood there looking at his car for a moment. He'd spent more on that Mercedes than most families earn in a year. He'd killed a dog with it recently and all he cared about was that the dealership couldn't fix it by the time he got off work.

What a waste this guy was. What a waste of humanity.

I turned around, walked back to the elevator, went to the ground floor, and found the security office Lester Tate had mentioned. The guard who had tried to get Graham to put out his cigar, the chubby young guy, sat alone at a table in front of a bank of video displays. I watched him prick his finger and squeeze a drop of blood into a testing unit.

I knocked on the open door. He looked up, startled.

"Sorry about that," I said. "It's just, there's no use arguing with a guy like him."

"Oh, I know." He squinted at the reading on the meter and said under his breath, "Time for a shot." And then, aloud, "I'm going to write him up. The fine for smoking in the building is pretty steep."

"It won't matter to him. It's pocket change."

"It doubles with every offence."

"It still won't matter."

"But I'm going to get it on the record."

The guard's name was Kenny. He showed me how to self-administer an insulin shot, told me he wanted to be a cop but couldn't pass the physical.

For half an hour, I rode shotgun as he drove the rounds of the Town Center. Maybe he thought I was just being a nice guy, but to be honest, I needed the company of a decent person to wash the bitter traces of Leighton Graham from my mind.

"Every time I start taking the weight off," Kenny told me as we passed the hospital lots, "I don't know... I go crazy and binge, and I wind up worse off than when I started."

He didn't live in his mom's basement. He shared an apartment with three other guys. He had a girlfriend and he wanted to propose to her. I could identify with that. It makes your nerves raw. What if she says no? What if, when you lay your soul on the line, she hesitates and you see how awkward she feels? You see her thinking through the words to let you down easy. What do you do with that future you'd envisioned? There is no next step, because you bet everything on one moment, one syllable, one yes.

"You have a ring?" I asked.

"Not yet. But even if I did..."

"What?"

"What kind of life could I give her?" Kenny seemed to deflate all at once. "She wants kids. When I put myself in her shoes, the question isn't, Do I love this man? I know she does. The question is, Am I willing to sign up for a life where we may never own a home? Never own a new car? What if the kids have health problems? How do we pay for that? Would you want to sign up for that kind of life?"

The way he looked at me then, I got the sense this was a dry run of the proposal and he was praying for someone to say yes, to quell his fears and give him courage.

But the way he phrased it, who could say yes to that? Why does a young guy with his whole life ahead of him in the richest country in the world have to think like that?

This is what I mean about people being troubled, the people I run into in the course of this job. You don't have to look for it. You don't have to dig. Just scratch the surface, and there it is.

"You have to think positive," I said. "Look for opportunities. Don't let your head get stuck in where you're at now. Things change."

12

At midnight, I was leaning against the door of my car in the lot beside Karl Larsson's office, watching a pair of headlights approach. That would be Lester Tate making the rounds in his Westwood patrol car.

He pulled to a stop ten feet in front of me, flipped on the brights to blind me, and I heard him get out of the car. I put my arm in front of my eyes to shield them, and I could just see his figure approaching from my right. He had a club in his hand, and his arm was half-raised, ready to swing.

"What's up, Lester?"

"Damn!" His arm relaxed. "What are you doing out here?"

"I wanted to follow up on a question."

A few things had bothered me when I'd spoken with him earlier that day. Why wouldn't he shut the door and come out into the yard to talk? It was a lot quieter out there. We could have wrapped up our conversation in half the time. It seemed like he wanted the distraction, wanted conversation to be difficult to prevent it from getting too deep.

And why, when I asked if he had anything more to tell me, had he looked away?

Naw. I ain't got nothing more to say about that.

A simple no would have sufficed.

He knew something more, but he didn't want to say it. And when he went inside at the end of our talk, he left the door wide open. A strange thing to do in the muggy, buggy August heat. I wondered if he did that because on some level, he wanted me to pursue him, wanted me to pull out of him the information he couldn't quite spill on his own.

Lester slid his club into a loop on his belt and said, "Let's take a ride."

The interior of his patrol car smelled like weed. It took me a minute to realize the smell was coming from his uniform. He checked his eyes in the rearview, red narrow slits, and muttered "Damn" under his breath.

"You okay to drive?" I asked.

"Hell yeah! I'm one with the wheel! This is the Buddha weed!"

He turned the car around and headed up the narrow, wooded road, gripping the wheel with the white-knuckle intensity of a fighter pilot heading into battle. The speedometer said we were going eight miles an hour.

"Detective, huh? Yeah, you knew I was holding out on you!" He turned and grinned at me. "I knew when I walked away. I knew like, damn, that dude is on to me. You know, it's like, some people get paranoid when they smoke weed? Well I'm the opposite. I get paranoid when I ain't smoked weed.

"See... see here? See this here?" He pointed toward an empty spot at the edge of the road.

"Motherfucker was parked here a minute ago when I drove down. It's kids, you know?" He turned and gave me a look. "It's these kids, they come down here and get high, drink beer, screw they girlfriend, whatever. I pass by, hang in the lot a couple minutes, then come back up and they gone. You feel me? You get what I'm saying? Cuz, it's like, I don't want to have to get out and talk to them dudes. Fuck, we out in the middle of the woods. I don't trust no one out here. I just pass by, hang out, give 'em a few minutes to leave, and when I come back out the lot, they gone, see? It's like an unwritten rule. It's like they vibe me. They get the fuck out and I ain't gotta—Hey, man, you hungry?"

"No."

"Me too. Let's hit the Wawa up the road."

"I want to ask you about last Sunday night."

"Yeah, I know. I'm hungry as fuck. This is the fucking Buddha weed and my mouth's so dry I need about a gallon of Gatorade."

The three-mile drive to the gas station took ten minutes. Lester was quiet through much of the ride, his attention focused on keeping the car between the yellow and white lines at a whopping twenty miles an hour.

Inside the Wawa, he grabbed a couple bottles of Gatorade and two hot dogs. I got a bottle of cold water, and we went back to the car.

"Too bright in there," Lester said, digging into hot dog number one.

We talked for half an hour. Not all of it was useful. I had a hard time keeping him on track, thanks to the Buddha weed.

"See, I thought about it after you left," he told me. "'Cause the police had come by already and asked the same questions, same questions about Sunday night you asked, and I told 'em the same thing. But see, you asked that one extra question at the end. Was there anything else I wanted to tell you? They didn't ask that.

"And I got to thinking, you know? I'm thinking this guy Larsson, he probably got a family. You feel me? He probably got someone at home worrying about him. So I think—" He turned and looked at me, a little nervous.

"I think... You keep this off the record, right? I mean, off the record, unless something come of it? I don't think nothing will come of it, 'cause Cade ain't the kind of guy who would hurt no one. He's too messed up himself."

"Who's Cade?"

"Dude in the parking spot. He ain't supposed to be in the building 'cause they fired his ass."

"What parking spot?"

"The one I showed you. In the woods. A hundred yards up from the building, where the kids like to park and get high."

"Cade was parked in that spot Sunday night?"

"That's what I'm saying, man. I wasn't supposed to let him in."

"You let him in? To the office?"

"Dude got fired, man. 'Cause he's a fucking dumbass. I mean, he's a decent guy, just not real bright."

It took me a while to back him up and get the whole story. Cade had worked at Westwood, on the night shift, like Lester Tate. They drove the same rounds. Cade had failed a drug test and had been fired a week before Karl Larsson disappeared.

"See, he's stupid, man. Westwood, they test. They test everyone. Piss test every six weeks. It ain't even random. You know it's coming. I got it right on my calendar, get a bottle of piss from my mom the night before. Weed is legal in Virginia, but not on this job."

"You use your mother's urine?"

"Only person I know who's a hundred percent clean. Woman ain't touched a drop of liquor in her life, much less weed, Oxy, coke, smack. Hardest drug she take is aspirin. And Westwood, they don't want to catch nobody. That's why they tell you when the test is. They don't even watch you go. Just hand you a cup and tell you to fill it. You could pour apple juice in there, I don't think they'd care.

"So how messed up does Cade have to be to screw that up? Dude just forgot. Walked in there and pissed out a quart of Roxies."

"Roxies? The opioids?"

"Yeah. He like 'em 'cause you can crush 'em up and snort 'em. Not like Oxies that got all that gummy stuff in 'em."

"Okay," I said, "so Cade got fired. Why was he parked in the woods by the office on Sunday night?"

"'Cause he left a bag of pills inside the building. His girl's hooked on those pills too, and he was hiding his stash. He keep 'em in the house and she'll take 'em all herself, you know?"

I remembered the office in the front of the building, with the cubbies and the Westwood jacket draped over the chair.

"In that room up front?" I asked.

"Yeah. Guy's pathetic, man. You ever seen someone dopesick? It's like the world's falling on them. It's like, I can't even look at them. That dude was begging like—"

Tate clicked his tongue and shook his head in pity. "Like he wasn't even a man. I told him, get inside and get your shit and get out."

"But you didn't tell the cops about that?"

"They didn't ask. They didn't say, Was a former employee parked up in the woods, and did you let him in to get his bag of pills? If they'd have asked me that, I would have told 'em straight up. And that would have got my ass fired. So I didn't tell nobody."

He brushed some relish from his uniform, crumpled the Wawa bag, and tossed it in the back seat. Then he checked the rearview and started backing out.

"Then you come along," he said. "Ask if there's anything else I want to tell you, and I start feeling bad about this Larsson dude. Dude might have kids and shit."

He put the car in drive and we pulled out onto the road.

"See now, if nothing come of this, you don't have to tell nobody I told you about Cade. Then it's no trouble for me. And if something does come of it, maybe you find Karl Larsson, and maybe I get fired, and maybe that's God's will. I accept that, you understand?"

"Yeah, I got you."

"You keep this to yourself?"

"For now."

We headed back along the dark, winding road toward Larsson's office.

"So Cade got his pills and left?" I said.

"Cade went into the office and crushed up a Roxy and started snorting. I took a walk around, saw Larsson, talked to him for a couple minutes so he wouldn't get up and wander around and accidentally find Cade all strung out up front."

"How long did you talk to Larsson?"

"Five minutes. Maybe a little more."

"What did you talk about?"

"Just shootin' the shit. Asked him what all that code was about on his computer screen. He told me it could figure out whether a person would succeed at a job. I don't know how they figure that. I don't even know myself when I'm gonna like a job."

I noticed a light just before the turn onto the wooded road that led to Larsson's office. A bare yellow bulb above the door of a small brick house. The house was so small, I hadn't noticed it in daylight. I made a note to come back later and talk to the occupant.

As we turned, I asked Lester Tate if Cade was gone when he left to continue his rounds.

"I thought he was. I checked the front room. He wasn't there. I drove out and saw his car was still parked there. He wasn't in it. Must have been in the bathroom."

"Is this guy dangerous?"

"Only to himself. Cade wouldn't hurt nobody. He ain't strong, he ain't mean, he's just strung out. Left his car right up here." He pointed to the spot as we passed. "Right up where that Explorer was sitting when I rolled in."

"What Explorer? Was it blue?"

"Yeah. Blue Explorer."

"With a dent in the back?"

"Yeah. You see it too?"

"No. When did you see a blue Explorer parked here?"

"Right when I rolled in tonight. Right before I drove up on you and shined my brights in your eyes."

Damn. The Explorer must have come in with its lights off. Otherwise, I would have seen it.

We were in the lot now, approaching my car.

"Did you get a look at who was inside?"

"Yeah. I put my spotlight on him. Dude didn't like that."

"What did he look like?"

"Like... who's that baseball player up in New York?"

"You gotta be more specific."

"Tall-ass dude. Hit like sixty homer runs last year."

"Aaron Judge?"

"That's the one. Only Judge smiles. This dude don't look real friendly. Or maybe he just don't like people shining a light in his face."

"So, like a light-skinned black guy?"

"Dude's mixed. He got some white in him."

"All right," I said. "What's Cade's last name?"

"Weller."

"You know where he lives?"

"Arlington, I think."

13

The next morning, I drove back to Loudon County and stopped at the little brick house I'd seen the night before. The house had a clear view of the road just before the turnoff to Karl's office. It was a long shot, but maybe whoever lived there had stayed up late on Sunday night looking out the window and writing down license plate numbers. Maybe they could give me the winning Mega Millions number too.

I parked in the gravel beside the house, behind a blue Chevy Spark and a red Bolt. The mold on the Spark told me it didn't get much use. The Bolt was clean and well kept, but I didn't see a charger anywhere, so it probably didn't belong to whoever lived there.

I walked up the front steps and got a pleasant surprise when I reached the top. The house had one of those video doorbells. It recorded every car that drove by.

I gave it a ring, and an old man inside told me to hold my horses, he was coming. It took him a while to get there, and when the door opened, I saw why. He was stooped and walked with a cane.

He asked if he could help me, but his tone told me he didn't much want to.

I told him I was investigating Karl Larsson's disappearance, and he told me the cops had already been by. They wanted the same thing I wanted. The doorcam video from Sunday night.

He turned and barked into the house, "Alexa! Give me the video from Sunday night!"

Did that work, I wondered? Can you really give your smart speaker such a vague instruction and expect it to understand? How could it know which video you were talking about? Maybe it would think you meant the video you watched on Netflix on Sunday night.

A woman in her midforties walked into the room behind the old man and said, "Dad, don't yell so loud. I don't have the video."

Then, to me she said, "We already gave it to the police."

"Loudon County?" I asked. "Or Fairfax?" We were in Loudon, but the investigation started in Fairfax, where Larsson lived and where Recursion had its offices.

"Fairfax," said Alexa.

"Okay." That meant Jim Burkheim had access to it, and if he had it and didn't tell me anything, there must not be much to see.

I thanked the people for their time and went to see Jim.

14

I found Jim in his janitor-closet office and he told me what I had expected. The video wasn't worth much. It had rained late Sunday afternoon, and a fog had settled in during the evening. Jim had edited the video down to show only the cars passing by between 7:00 p.m. Sunday, just before Larsson drove in, and 8:00 a.m. Monday, when workers started returning to the office.

We saw Larsson's Mazda pass by at 7:37, when it was still light out. The fog thickened after dark, and every car that passed was just a grey ghost chasing the halo of its headlights.

"There's nothing of use here," Jim said. "Plenty of cars, but you can't tell the color, make, or model, much less get a license plate. You want a copy of this?"

I told him I did. He plugged a thumb drive into his computer and loaded it up with video while he told me about his retirement plans. There was a resort down in Mexico with an all-you-can-eat buffet and free drinks. He was going to start his retirement there with a two-week stay.

"Maybe I'll meet a nice lady friend on the beach and have a little adventure."

I don't know what kind of woman goes to a resort alone looking to hook up with a 250-pound middle-aged alcoholic, but who am I to deprive a man of his dreams?

"Sounds like a fun couple of weeks," I said. "What about the next twenty years after that? Don't you worry about getting bored?"

"Nah. Between baseball season, football season, and basketball season, I'm pretty much covered. Plus, I'm going to start smoking."

"Cigarettes?"

He laughed. "Meat. I'm getting a smoker out in the yard. Make some brisket."

I could see him out there with a twelve-pack or two, watching the smoke rise for four hours while he listened to the Nationals game on the radio. For a second, I had this nasty thought, a flash of Leighton Graham–style thinking. How could someone aim so low and be content? Was Jim *that* burnt out by life? Is this what years of heavy drinking did to a man?

"You should marry Claire," he said.

"I know."

"Because, you know why? Because you're going to get old no matter what, and you can do it with someone, or you can do it alone, and alone is a hard way to go."

"You should take your own advice, Jim. Why didn't you remarry after your wife left?"

"I liked my freedom." He plucked the thumb drive from the computer and handed it to me. "I liked it till I had too much of it, and then I didn't know what to do with myself. And you know what, Freddy? Soon I'll have a lot more freedom, and it scares the shit out of me. It really does. Some people look forward to a long retirement. I don't think I'm gonna hang around too long. I don't want to. You should get married, Freddy. Claire's a beautiful woman. And she's smart as hell. A smart woman will keep her man from doing dumb things. Remember that."

15

Jim's words didn't sway me one way or the other. If I hadn't bought the ring that day, I would have bought it the next. I'd been thinking this through for weeks, and I never once wavered on the decision. I asked myself the same question from a thousand different angles, to see if there was any hint of doubt anywhere, but the answer was always firm.

Did I want to wake up to Claire every day for the rest of my life? If you had asked that question a year ago, if you had phrased it as "Could you even stand waking up to the same person, any person, every day for the rest of your life," I would have given you a resounding no. I'd been married once, and ever since then, I'd been glad to not be married.

The thing with Miriam was, we just drifted into it. We started dating, we hit it off in bed. It seemed like a good thing, but once we tied the knot, we couldn't seem to hit it off outside of bed, and that's where people spend most of their time.

My job certainly didn't help. How can you have a stable home life when you don't even know when you'll be home? When you have to travel at a moment's notice, sometimes for days on end? How can you be calm and pleasant and fun to be around when your job is to root out liars and cheaters and thieves?

Think what kind of mood you'd be in if you had to follow people around and watch them steal, watch them cheat on their spouses, day in and day out. And then you have to go back to the person who hired you and tell them, yeah, that employee you trust so much is ripping you off. Your husband is screwing his intern, the blonde one who's only six years older than your daughter.

How do you think a daily grind of that affects your world view? And then there are guys like Graham. Sometimes the ones paying you are worse than the ones you're investigating.

It all adds up. The grouchy detective comes home to his lonely, hot-tempered wife—two people who never learned how to talk to each other—and what you have is a mess.

So I've asked myself, do I really want to get into this again? Do I really want to risk putting Claire through a life like that? I mean, if I love the woman, I want her to be happy.

She has her issues with it too, with marriage. She walked out on her one serious boyfriend when she learned he was going to propose. Walked out without a word and moved to a different city. That's how much it freaked her out.

She's grown since then. She's had to face a lot of things, and I don't think she'd run out on me. But the two things we can't talk about are marriage and kids. We'll get there. We're inching toward it, and we can talk about anything else. I do mean anything. I've told her things I've never told another soul. She's told me things too.

I bought the ring because I'd looked at a thousand of them, and this one was *her*. She doesn't wear much jewelry, and the little she does wear isn't showy. But look closely, and you'll see the quality.

I got her platinum with finely carved filigree and a brilliant cut diamond, flawless, color D, which is the highest clarity. It's not a big rock. I went for quality over size. She'll appreciate that, though she won't be seeing it any time soon.

I don't know when the right time will be, but I know that when it comes, I have the right ring for the right woman. And

I'm a little older and a little wiser than I was the first time around. I know how *not* to be a husband.

I put the ring in my pocket, ate lunch at a sandwich shop, and called Cade Weller four times. I got his number from Westwood, his former employer, but he wouldn't answer. Maybe he'd been up all night snorting Roxies.

I decided I'd swing by his apartment and wake him up.

16

Cade Weller and his girlfriend, Jennifer, lived in a ground floor apartment in a dump of a house off Route 29 in Arlington. The apartment, a converted garage attached to a single-story house, still had a driveway leading up to it. The rest of the house, which was a separate unit with a separate mailbox, might have been two bedrooms, max. Whoever lived there kept the place just clean enough to keep the neighbors from complaining.

Weller's apartment had a single window looking out to the street. The top half of the front door was glass, so you could see who was knocking without having to open it. Cheap white blinds hung behind the window and the door glass, keeping the world and daylight out. I could hear a man and woman fighting inside as I approached.

I tapped on the glass, loud enough for them to hear without sounding too forceful. The voices quieted immediately. If Weller and his girlfriend were both using, as Lester Tate had told me, they might be used to visits from people they didn't want to see. Cops, or dealers collecting money, or other users desperately looking for someone who had a stash.

Jennifer answered, pale and unhealthy looking, with dry skin and dry black hair and bags beneath her eyes. Her shirt was torn, and she was holding it shut with one hand to keep from exposing her chest.

"What?"

"Is Cade in?"

"No. Who are you?"

"Don't tell me he's not here. I just heard a man's voice."

She flung the door open and yelled, "Cade! Someone's here to kick your ass!"

I stepped inside before she could change her mind and shut me out. She left the door open, giving me enough light to see the dopesickness Tate had described. Cade Weller, black-haired, pale and sniffling, had watery blue eyes. He wiped his nose and blinked at me, a little unsteady on his feet.

"Who are you?"

I told him my name and that I was an investigator. Before I could get any further, he cut me off. "You have a car?"

"Yeah. You need to go somewhere?"

"Yeah," Jennifer shouted. "He needs to get the fuck out of here, which he could do if he had his own car, but he doesn't, because he wrecked it."

"Can you give me a ride into DC?" Cade asked.

I told him I'd give him a ride if he would talk to me about Sunday night, and he said that was fine. I told him I was going to check him for weapons before he got into the car, and he was fine with that too. So far, I agreed with Lester Tate's assessment that Cade wasn't capable of hurting anyone. He was short and rail thin and looked weak from too much dope and too little food. A lot of junkies would rather get high than eat.

"Let me get my shoes," he said.

While he puttered in circles like a lost old man, Jennifer badgered him.

"Where's the money, Cade? You said we were going to be rich. Where's the fucking money? Now you don't even have a car!"

Christ! This would be Miriam and me if we'd had a drug problem.

"When's all the cash going to come rolling in?" she demanded. "Huh, Cade? Answer me, you junkie!"

She smacked his shoulder. Not hard. She put just enough behind it to get his attention, but he ignored her. He picked up one shoe off the floor, a white Chuck Taylor All Star, and slid it onto the wrong foot.

Jennifer turned to me and said, "Cade's going to be rich. Cade's going to have a fortune any day now."

"How's that?" I asked.

Cade got the shoe onto the right foot and then puttered around looking for its mate.

"I don't know," Jennifer said. "How are you getting this fortune you keep talking about?"

"Shut up," said Cade.

"Don't bother checking his pockets," Jennifer said. "Cade's money is all in his head."

She turned and pulled off the torn shirt and I could see the vertebrae poking from her spine as she bent and yanked a dingy white t-shirt from the floor. She pulled it on as Cade found a second Chuck Taylor, only this one was black.

He walked past me, out the door, with the second shoe in hand.

"Come on, let's go."

I followed him down the driveway, Jennifer slamming the door behind us, as Cade hopped on one foot while attempting to slide the black Chuck onto the other foot. It was more than he could pull off. He fell on his face, and Jennifer opened the door to say "Ha!" before slamming it again.

Where did Cade want to go? To a corner in Southeast DC where guys like Cade went to get well for a few hours, before they inevitably got sick again.

17

Cade Weller confirmed Lester Tate's story as we crossed the Roosevelt Bridge into DC. He failed his piss test with flying colors.

"Hell, I was high when I took it. Half the piss went on the floor."

He'd been fired after the results came back. He and Jennifer burned through whatever pills they had, and then he went out to Karl Larsson's office to retrieve the stash he'd hidden behind the cubbies in the front office.

Only he couldn't get in, because Westwood had made him turn in his access card. So he parked and waited for Lester, then begged his way in. He crushed some pills and snorted them and went into the bathroom, where he dozed off for a while.

"How long?" I asked.

"I don't know. Sleeping's a waste of a high."

"You don't know how long you were in there?"

"Nope."

"Was it light or dark when you left?"

"Dark. I wasn't out *that* long. I could still feel the Roxy pretty strong when I woke up. Had a ring around my ass too."

"You fell asleep on the toilet?"

"Why do people get so hung up on that? Like you never do?"

I didn't see the point in telling him I was able to maintain consciousness through a bowel movement. I felt like that would be rubbing it in.

We were rolling down Independence Avenue, past the monuments and the polo grounds and the hordes of sweaty tourists on a fine August afternoon, and all he wanted was to obliterate his mind and send the green grass and the big shade trees and the deep blue sky into oblivion.

"You see anyone when you were out there?"

"Who would I see?" he asked.

"Karl Larsson."

"Didn't see him."

His answer came back a little too quick.

"You sure?"

"Dude, I'm sure. I didn't see anyone at all."

"Bullshit," I said. "You saw Lester Tate. He let you in."

"Yeah, well Lester doesn't count."

It's hard to know when an addict is lying. Some of the ones I've known lie for no reason at all. I didn't believe Cade Weller.

"When we get up on The Hill," he said, "stay right. Follow Pennsylvania Avenue. I'll show you where to go after that."

The place he directed me to was not a place I liked to go. I'd been down there in the past, but only for work, and I was always happier to leave than to arrive.

"Here," he said, pointing to a huddle of young guys on the corner.

"I'm not stopping here," I told him.

"No, you don't pull up in front. That'll piss 'em off. Drive past. We'll walk back."

I drove past and told him I wasn't walking anywhere. I was scanning the block, making an inventory of everyone in sight.

"Yo, pull up, man. Pull up." He thumped the dash above the glovebox.

"Not here." I didn't like the looks of the guy on the corner up ahead. A lookout for the dealers, maybe, or maybe someone just looking out for an opportunity.

"Dude!" Cade jerked my arm and the car took a sharp right into the curb. "Here! You gotta stop *here!*"

I had to hit the brakes to keep from blowing a tire against the curb.

"Don't grab my arm when I'm driving. What's the matter with you?"

"Yo, you have any cash?" He yanked the glovebox open.

"Not for you." I slammed it shut.

And then the trouble started. If this idiot hadn't got me so distracted, I would have seen it coming.

There was one guy on his side of the car, one guy on mine. Both had guns. Cade's guy was calm and kept the gun pointed at his chest. My guy was agitated. A blond, scraggly-haired kid who looked like he might have come from the richer suburbs before taking a wrong turn in life. I could tell from the scabs on his face, from the rotting teeth and dilated pupils, he was on meth and beyond reason.

He banged his gun against the window, telling me he wanted it down, while the guy on the other side stepped back to let Cade out of the car.

I rolled down my window.

"Hand it over, motherfucker!" The meth head was waving his gun in my face.

I pulled my wallet from my back pocket and handed it to him.

"Phone too," he said, shaking. He twitched so much, I was worried he'd blow my brains out by accident.

I grabbed the phone from between the seats and handed it to him. Cade was face-down on the sidewalk. A third guy— new to the scene—frisked him head to toe while the gunman stood over and kept watch.

"And the pocket," my guy shouted. "Gimme what's in your pocket."

He meant the box. The box with Claire's ring.

"Fuck you," I said. That ring was for one person only. It was hers, first and always and forever, and no punk-ass thief was ever going to lay a hand on it.

That was the stupidest thing I'd ever said, and I meant it with all my heart.

"What'd you say?" The kid was twitching and shaking, his gun just inches from my eye.

"I said it's yours." And when I handed it to him, I felt like I was giving up my soul, like part of me just died. I don't even remember the guy running off.

I turned and saw Cade's frisker dragging him by the ankle. Cade was holding on, not wanting to give up his cash. The guy finally pulled it from Cade's sock, then he and the gunman bolted.

Cade started crying, bawling like a toddler who'd lost his candy, bawling over fifty bucks that might have kept him high the rest of the day. He had fought those guys and risked his life for a measly fifty bucks! However rash I had been, it had been on account of love. At least, that's what I was thinking when the words came out. Cade was just as rash, and maybe his love was just as deep. Or maybe we were both sick.

"Get in the car," I shouted.

Cade dusted himself off and started walking.

I drove alongside and shouted, "Where the hell are you going?"

"I know a dude around the corner who will front me."

Idiot!

I took off.

18

It took me an hour to stop shaking. I'd been robbed before. I'd been shot before. Neither one is something you get used to.

Later that afternoon, I drove back out to Cade's apartment in Arlington. He wasn't there, but Jennifer was. She was calmer now, because she was high. While Cade was out risking his life—risking our lives—in DC, she stayed home and dug out whatever stash she'd been hiding from him.

We sat with the door open and I asked her a few questions about Cade while she smoked cigarettes and occasionally nodded off. I wanted to know if he had told her anything about the night he'd gone out to Karl's office. Did she even know he'd gone?

"Yeah, I knew. He was supposed to bring home some pills. He brought home, like, two. And he was high as fuck, so I know what he did with the rest."

"What time did he get home?"

"Oh, man, it was like four."

"Four in the morning?"

"Yeah. That pissed me off. He said he'd be back by midnight. I was climbing the walls."

"Did he say anything to you about being out there?"

"Said he saw Lester."

"Anyone else?"

"Yeah, there was a guy working at a desk."

"Larsson?"

She shrugged. "And the guy he was talking to."

"He was talking to Lester," I said. Tate had told me that himself.

"No, after Lester left. The Larsson guy was talking to someone else."

"You mean, like, on the phone?"

"No. A guy was there in the building with him. At his desk, talking."

"Do you know who?"

"Dude! How could I possibly know..."

She nodded off again, then awoke with a jerk as her chin hit her chest.

"Do you know when Cade might be back?" I asked.

She shook her head. "I never know when he's coming back. And now he has no car."

At last I had a solid lead. Cade Weller had information about another witness, one who had been talking to Larsson just before his disappearance but had not come forward. All I had to do was find Cade Weller and get him to talk. *All*, I thought. As if those were easy tasks. As if any aspect of dealing with an opioid addict was easy.

I gave Jennifer my card and told her to call me when she knew where Cade was.

When I got up to leave, she stood and walked me to the door.

The sky had clouded over and rain was on its way, and a blue Ford Explorer with a dent in the rear was parked across the street, and I didn't like the looks of the guy inside.

19

He saw me coming. I was coming straight for him, and Jennifer stood in the doorway and watched.

And he got out, and he was about six foot two and lean, with the kind of muscle that's God given, not gym inflated. I learned to be wary of them in my boxing days because they can get a lot of power on their punches. Lester Tate was right. The guy did look like Aaron Judge. Mixed race, blue-green eyes, short-cropped hair.

He wore a fitted shirt and fitted sweatpants with gathers at the ankles, and when he got out and shut the door, he turned around, and I could see there was no gun tucked into the waistband at the small of his back. There was no gun on his sides or down at his ankles, and nothing in his pockets except maybe a tube of lip balm.

He had this cocky look of unshakable confidence, complete self-assurance. The kind you usually only see in guys who are carrying and willing to shoot. But he had no weapon—his clothes were too fitted to conceal anything—so what the hell was he so cocky about?

"You've been following me," I said. "Why?"

"I wanted to see where you went."

The guy had bad intent; I could smell it. I heard Jennifer shut the door of the house behind me as the first drops of rain splatted down on the pavement. She shut herself in and shut trouble out so she could enjoy the rest of her high.

If the guy was a private investigator, he sure was being a dick about it, following me around for three days and now giving me that nasty glare. I wanted to ask him who he was working for, but you can't really expect an investigator to answer that. We treat our clients with the same confidentiality they expect from lawyers and doctors.

So I asked him, "You working the Larsson case?"

He shook his head, and it wasn't a friendly no. It was a I-don't-answer-to-you shake of the head. It was a don't even ask because you're not getting anything out of me kind of look. I think the guy was pissed off because he'd screwed up. He was following me and he got caught cold. That's a stupid, rookie mistake. Parking so close—that was an amateur move, and the way his eyes bore into me, I could tell he was mad, like he wanted to punish me for a mistake that was obviously his fault.

Only he was more than mad. Animals can sense violent intent, and he was an animal about to attack, and I was an animal tuned-in to a very bad vibe, like a dog with its hackles up. I didn't know why in hell this guy would want to fight me. In my ring days, my opponents didn't want to fight me, even though they were pros and they were getting paid. *I* wouldn't want to fight me, but if I did, I'd be nervous, and this guy wasn't scared, and that's what put me off. He just stood there with his fists balled at his sides.

Finally, I decided I was going to throw first, because this guy wasn't going to move away, and I felt like if I tried to back off, he'd take a swing and he might clip me.

I threw a left jab and he dodged it exactly the way I expected him to, down and to his left. I knew exactly where his head would be and I timed a crushing right follow-up that smashed the back of his skull into the driver side window and shattered it, and that cocky motherfucker crumpled to the ground, and so did I.

I went down in slow motion. Like, crazy slow. The guy never even hit me. He didn't even swing. But I went down on my face, and then I drifted up through the clouds, and then the world went black.

And then I was awake, and my legs were wobbly and my guts were ready to heave and my head and heart were full of bliss. I stepped over the guy and staggered past the parked cars until I fell again.

The next time I woke up, I was in a bush at the side of a house and it was dark, and it was raining, and my clothes were soaked through.

How long had I been there? It had to have been hours.

I got up and still wasn't steady on my feet. I walked back onto the street and the cocky guy was gone, and the blue Explorer was gone, and the lights were out in Jennifer's apartment.

I got into my car and started the engine, and something was beeping at me. It took forever to figure out what.

My seatbelt wasn't fastened, that's what.

I had the sense to realize I was in no condition to drive, so I cut the engine, and it's a good thing I did, because a minute later, I was asleep again.

The next time I awoke, it was dawn, and the sky had cleared.

I drove home. No wallet, no phone, no ring for Claire. I got in the shower and saw this little thing sticking out of what looked like a pimple on my left forearm.

I got out of the shower, got a magnifying glass and some tweezers and pulled a tiny piece of steel from the middle of the red welt.

The thing in the guy's pocket, what I thought was a tube of lip balm, was a syringe. He'd stuck me with it when I threw the left, stuck it right into my left forearm, where it broke off, probably before it could deliver its full payload.

What if it hadn't broken? What if he'd gotten ten drops of that stuff into my bloodstream instead of one or two?

I'd be dead.

I'd be dead without even knowing what happened. Claire would fly back from her trip and Ed would tell her the news, and then what would her life be like? She loved me as much as I loved her.

I stood at the sink and asked myself, is it worth it to live like this? Is any job worth this kind of risk?

When I was younger, I would have said, "Yeah, sure. Life is a risk. You roll with it." I didn't care too much for myself in those days. And I was single. If I disappeared, who would notice?

Now the question was, was it even responsible to work a job where I was putting my son's father at risk? Where I was putting Claire's boyfriend, maybe Claire's husband at risk?

I didn't know. I really didn't know anymore.

But it definitely wasn't worth taking that kind of risk for a guy like Leighton Graham.

20

I went to Best Buy on 14th Street and picked up a new phone. It took a while to set up my number—I had to tell them my old phone had been stolen—and to get all my apps and settings back. The fact that it's even possible is a miracle of technology, like restoring the spirit of the deceased into a new body.

I got out of there around 11:00 a.m. and headed straight for Reston. Graham had left a message about me not showing up for yesterday's 6:00 p.m. meeting.

"Not very professional, Mr. Ferguson. And not very nice to keep me waiting."

Funny how he calls me Mr. Ferguson when he wants to be condescending. If the situation had been reversed, if a reliable professional had unexpectedly failed to appear for a meeting, the first thing on my mind would be, I hope you're okay.

I guess I'm not cut out to be a corporate axe man. I can scratch that from my list of alternative careers if I ever do decide to quit this game.

As I drove along Route 267, I thought through the report I'd give Graham. I'd skip the robbery in DC. He didn't need to know about that. In fact, I could picture his smirk when he heard that part of the story. I knew what he'd be thinking. Tough guy Freddy, professional detective, got roughed up and ripped off by a drug-addled kid. Now he has to go to DMV and get a new license. And then I pictured his nose bleeding all over his pretty white shirt after I'd popped him one.

No, I'd keep the robbery out of it.

I'd also skip the part about my confrontation with Explorer Guy, though I would tell him the guy had been following me. Omitting the altercation meant omitting the part about why I didn't show up. I didn't make the meeting because I was asleep in a bush in someone's side yard, getting rained on. If he asked why I didn't show up, I'd just tell him flat out, "I don't like you, Leighton."

That made me laugh.

The only material lead I'd gotten was Jennifer's statement that Cade had seen someone talking to Larsson in the office just before Larsson's disappearance. I wasn't ready to tell him about that either. Hearsay from a junkie that she claims to have heard from another junkie is not exactly reliable evidence.

I needed to find Cade and hear his account, but I had no idea where he was, and he probably didn't either. There was a more reliable way to verify the presence of another person. Larsson's building had a card scanner by the entrance. You have to scan to get in, and your card reports your identity to some computer somewhere.

If someone scanned in, there would be a record of it. There was always the chance that Larsson had let them in, in which case there would be no scan. But it was worth a shot. I called Graham's assistant and left a message asking for a record of who had scanned in and out of that building that night. I was sure the cops and the company itself had already reviewed those records, but I had to cover my bases.

And if there was no scan, if Larsson had let the person in, it must have been someone he knew and trusted. I could narrow that down to a fairly small circle and then start interviewing people.

I was just coming off the Town Center exit ramp when the radio gave me a jolt of unexpected news. Karl Larsson had been found dead in his car within the past hour, in the woods about a mile and a half from his office. Police said there was no sign of foul play.

I let out a long sigh of frustration and disappointment. I wanted the guy to be alive, to go home to his wife and give her some support and continue chiseling away at his debts. I wanted him and Erica to take that vacation they'd talked about, to buy the new house they'd been looking at.

The frustration part— Well I can sum that up in one sentence. I'd put my life on the line for Leighton Graham, a guy I wouldn't even want to have a beer with.

How much had I made on this job? Three days at double the usual rate. No, four days. I would count today. Four days of abuse from Graham, an armed robbery, and a near murder. Plus the bonus of Cade Weller's delightful company.

When I thought about it that way, McDonalds didn't look like such a bad alternative to PI work. You show up, do your work, then leave. When you're off the clock, your mind is free. You don't waste time agonizing over your customers' lives or if there's a better way to flip a burger. Every two weeks, they give you money. Simple, right?

So why does my life have to be so complicated?

Because I chose this. Because, I don't know, I guess I like to make things hard for myself.

I pulled into the parking garage for my last meeting with Leighton Graham.

21

The meeting went about as expected.

"How hard could it be," he asked, "to find a guy just a mile and a half from where he disappeared? You could have walked it in half an hour. You're not very good at your job, are you, Freddy?"

You'd think a guy would be upset to hear that his coworker and old friend had just been found dead. But Leighton Graham wasn't one to dwell on difficult feelings. He preferred to puff himself by putting me down.

I remembered a clause in our contract. We would bill additional resources, like Claire, Bethany, Leon, or Ed, at double the hourly rate. None of them had worked this case, but I did discuss it with Claire over dinner. So I decided I'd add an hour of her time to the bill.

"What the hell happened to you yesterday that you couldn't show up for a damn meeting?" Graham was sitting on the edge of his desk. "Were you out getting drunk or something? You look like shit."

I changed it to two hours of Claire's time.

But he was right. I did look like shit. I still felt slow from whatever Explorer Guy had poked me with.

I asked Graham if the cops had given him any more information than what I'd heard on the radio. He gave me the lowdown as he paced in front of the window.

Larsson had left the office late Sunday night or early Monday morning; the cops still didn't have an exact time. He turned right off the office access road, drove a mile or so, and then drifted off the road at low speed. The cops think he may have been trying to pull over at the time. He lost consciousness and rolled through about two hundred feet of brush before his car came to rest against a tree.

What happened? They didn't know. Maybe he had a heart attack or a stroke. Or maybe he'd just popped a Percocet for his back pain and then got sleepy. The autopsy would tell.

"You talk to Erica?" I asked him.

"Thanks for reminding me."

The guy hadn't even thought of it.

"Send me your bill, Freddy. And don't bother with the final report. I don't need it. Consider yourself fired."

And that was it. That was the end.

The anticlimax left me so deflated, I didn't even feel like smashing Graham's car as I left the garage. That pretty Mercedes that cost almost as much as a damn condo.

I stopped by Erica's house to give my condolences. It was a sad scene. Barely lunchtime and she already had the wine box out.

But how was a person supposed to cope at a time like this? She told me the boys were on their way home from college. No one was taking it well.

In my mind, I registered another strike against my job. I'd been through this kind of scene before, more times than most people, and I'd go through it again. The hardest part is seeing another person's pain and not being able to take it away, not being able to fix it.

In bed a few weeks ago, Claire read me this passage from the Aeneid. Aeneas goes to the underworld and finds this enormous saltwater river. It's miles wide and miles long, and he says to his guide, "I didn't think there was so much water in all the world. Where does it come from?"

And his guide says, "It comes from the tears of the people in the world above."

22

Claire returned the following evening. We went to a Thai restaurant and she gave me the lowdown on her case. Turns out the wife *was* cheating.

"So her guy," she said over a spring roll appetizer, "shows up at the conference in Indianapolis. The two of them go right to bed."

"I guess that's what you do when you don't get to see your lover much."

"Then they go out to dinner, act cordial, no shows of affection, because they both know some of the other attendees and they don't want word to get around. Then back to the bedroom."

"His room, or hers?"

"Hers."

She told me neither one of them attended a single meeting or presentation. They both went and collected swag—flyers and buttons and tote bags and thumb drives—to prove to their spouses they'd attended.

"Wait," I said. "He's married too?"

"Yeah." Claire ordered a second glass of wine and asked if I wanted any. I put my hand over my glass. When the entrees arrived, she told me the rest.

"In Chicago, they didn't even go to the conference. He's from there. They went right to his house."

"Where was the guy's wife?"

"Out of town. Maybe at a conference of her own. She could have a boyfriend too."

"What's the point of getting married in the first place," I asked, "if you're going to carry on like that?"

"I know, right?" She picked up a mouthful of pad thai with her chopsticks and resumed her story.

"The thing that gets me," she said, "was this guy was exactly like her husband. He's money-oriented, he has a high opinion of himself. He's not very deep. You know the type I'm talking about?"

"Do I! I have no interest in seeing the likes of him again."

I told myself if this case had a bright spot, that was it. Leighton Graham would fade from being a daily presence to an old, bad memory.

Claire's presence was already improving my mood. This was what I meant about us lifting each other up without trying. Here I'd been brooding for a couple of days about my career choice, about having to deal with guys like Graham and Cade Weller and Explorer Guy, and then Claire comes back and talks about her work, and even though it's no more uplifting than mine, she has this energy and freshness when she talks about it. Engage this woman's mind and you see the life force glow in her.

"What I don't get," she said, "is why she'd cheat on her husband with a guy who's exactly like him. If you're going to go to all that trouble, why not choose some variety? The marriage obviously isn't working, so why pick a guy just like the one you don't like?"

"Maybe she does love her husband," I said. "Maybe she's seeking the attention he doesn't give her."

"Or maybe she's just stuck," Claire replied. "You know, like psychologists say people get stuck on some relationship that didn't work out in the past, and they keep recreating it because

A, it's familiar, and B, they want to be able to finally resolve it."

I had thought about that a number of times. When I was a kid, my dad used to beat me savagely. I hated violent men and swore I'd never become one.

And then what did I drift into? What decision did I make without even realizing I was making it?

I became a boxer. I made a career out of beating the crap out of big violent men—for money. In front of cheering crowds. I had made a spectacle of what I secretly hated, and I'd put myself right in the middle of the drama. And the irony of it didn't occur to me until after I'd retired. Or I should say, after I'd been forced out of the sport by a crooked manager.

I think I did "resolve" the issue, though, as Claire put it. Ever since I got shot down in Texas, I haven't had the same kind of anger, that unprovoked anger that swirls around inside all the time.

"Your case," Claire said, "turned into a kind of..."

"Tragedy?"

"I was going to say disappointment, but your word is better. Any idea what happened to Karl Larsson?"

"He had some kind of medical emergency. A heart attack or stroke. Or he took too much Percocet. He tried to pull over and lost it before he could nail the brake and put it in park. Just kind of rolled through the brush until he hit a tree. It wasn't a hard hit either. Not even enough to pop the airbags."

I'd learned that from Jim Burkheim at the Fairfax County PD.

"Larsson was taking Percocet?"

"Yeah. That might have made him sleepy, but it wouldn't have killed him. The stuff's just not that strong. You mind if we change the subject?"

"Yeah. No, sorry. I didn't mean to talk shop on date night. What did you do with your day off today?"

I let out a groan.

"What? You must have done something enjoyable. Bethany said you weren't in the office."

"No. I was down at the DMV, getting a new license. And then arguing with some jackass city clerk about re-issuing my investigator's license. And then hours on the phone cancelling all my credit cards and getting new ones."

"You lost your wallet?"

"Yeah."

"That's not like you, Freddy."

I didn't want to tell her I'd been robbed. She'd worry. She might start thinking what I'd been thinking, that maybe this isn't the best job for a man who's found a woman he wants to spend a long, long time with.

"Did you cut yourself?" She pointed to the bandage on my left forearm covering the near-fatal needle prick.

"It's nothing," I said.

I felt like I was sinking again. That damn ring! I'd be paying for it for the next twelve months, while some punk-ass meth addict had probably inhaled the money he'd got for it in ten minutes.

"You seem kind of down, Freddy."

"Sorry," I said. "I don't like to bring this stuff home, but sometimes I do."

The playful spark in her eyes told me she could help me forget about all this after dinner. And she did.

23

At breakfast the next morning, Claire slid her iPad across the table and said, "See that?"

We were at her place. The table was in the same area as the kitchen. She was eating oatmeal and blueberries and drinking tea in her blue silk pajamas. I was on my fourth slice of toast and second cup of coffee, already dressed for work.

"What am I looking at?" I asked her.

"Substack. Independent journalism."

It was an article about some company I never heard of.

"Check the byline," she suggested.

"Nazari Khan. Who's he?"

"Remember I told you they'd fire him?"

"No. Refresh my mind."

"Remember, he was the reporter with the deep contacts? The one writing all those dire warnings about how Recursion Talent was going to miss its earnings targets by a thousand miles?"

"What about him?"

"He's on Substack now."

I told her I didn't know what that meant, so she explained.

"A lot of top reporters are going there. They can write about whatever they want and they get paying subscribers. The money goes straight to the writer."

"Okay." I shrugged. "So how does that concern me?" I slid the iPad back across the table.

"I'm just saying," she said. "I predicted it, and I was right. That one reporter, Khan, almost singlehandedly tanked Recursion's stock. Just about everything he wrote turned out to be wrong, and the paper fired him. Now he's striking out on his own on Substack."

"Good for him," I said.

She gave me an irritated look.

"What?" I asked.

"How many cups of coffee does it take for you to stop being a grouch?"

"Sorry. I didn't realize."

"You need a new case to point your mind in a different direction."

She was right. And I got one the next day. Another missing person, only this one was easy and it had a happy ending.

A rich kid, twenty-one years old, from Montgomery County, goes out to Vegas, wins a ton of money and then disappears. He's supposed to start his senior year of college in a few weeks, and his parents want me to track him down.

It took me five days. The kid burned through sixty thousand dollars in Vegas, then had a religious experience in the Nevada desert with four prostitutes and a bag of magic mushrooms. He ended up on a New Age commune in Northern California.

From there, I got him into a psychiatric clinic where he was doing well. The guys on the commune said he had gotten too much enlightenment too fast and needed to get grounded again. The doctors said he was suffering from temporary psychosis from 120 consecutive hours on mind-altering drugs. He also had gonorrhea. Both, they said, would clear up with proper treatment. Unlike enlightenment, which I understand is terminal.

The case did snap me out of my funk. Vegas and Northern California were a nice change of scene. And no one on that case was as messed up or unpleasant as some of the people I'd encountered on the job for Leighton Graham.

Still, a few ghosts of the Larsson case popped up. The DC cops got in touch with me about Cade Weller, who'd been found dead with a needle in his arm not far from where we'd been robbed. The time of death was about twenty-four hours after I'd last seen him. It didn't surprise me.

How'd they know to contact me? His girlfriend told them I'd been out at their place asking questions.

The DC cops wanted to know if there was anything to follow up on there. I told them no, Cade was a long-time junkie with a one-track mind who had finally reached his destination. It was a closed case.

Graham's secretary, Nettie Hernandez, conscientious as she was, actually responded to my inquiry about who had scanned into the building the night Larsson disappeared. The answer was nobody. Just Larsson and a security guard named Lester Tate.

If Cade Weller really had seen someone in the office that night, he took that info to the grave.

Jim Burkheim from Fairfax County PD told me the preliminary report on Larsson's death said it was respiratory arrest. They found an unmarked bottle of pills in his car containing tablets that looked like Percocet but actually contained fentanyl. A lethal dose in each tablet.

I remembered Larsson's wife telling me that she held on to the pills because Larsson didn't trust himself with any drugs. Sounds like he had good reason to be wary. Burkheim figured Larsson had gone through his legitimate prescription, liked the pills a little too much, and then bought more on the internet or maybe even on the street.

"The street-bought stuff is usually counterfeit," Burkheim said. "Ditto for the internet. You get fentanyl because it's cheap and easy to manufacture and the guys who make it are no scientists. You're just as likely to get a lethal dose as anything else."

Burkheim knew about the financial strain Larsson had been under, and understood how a guy in that position might want to check out now and then. Maybe the pills let him feel, just for a few hours here and there, that the world didn't have him by the throat.

And then there was Jennifer, Cade Weller's junkie girlfriend. I'd left her my card and told her to call when Cade showed up. She called the day I got back from California, left an angry message about my friend beating her up.

She wasn't high. She was just agitated, probably from *not* being high, and her message didn't make a whole lot of sense. What friend of mine would beat her up? Ed? Leon? Bethany?

I deleted the message. As soon as she got high again, she'd forget that crazy talk.

24

Claire and I took the train from Union Station to New York for a weekend getaway. We'd racked up enough hotel points from work-related travel to get a free room at the Hilton in midtown.

We saw *Hamilton* at The Rodgers Theater, paid a visit to the Metropolitan Museum, and did a whole lot of walking in Central Park. I don't have good memories of that city, and to this day, I still look over my shoulder when I walk those streets.

Claire had a different set of memories, of being a workaholic in a city that rewarded work. She earned a lot of money but started enjoying work less and less. She moved in with a guy and then ran away when he wanted to tie the knot.

"I had a lot of growing to do," she said over dinner at a French restaurant that I thought was overpriced and too noisy.

The service was good though.

Halfway through the meal, she leaned in and said, "Why do you keep looking at the waiter?"

"He looks exactly like Karl Larsson," I said. "Like the photo Graham Leighton handed me the day I walked into his office. I mean, he looks like Larsson maybe ten years younger and twenty pounds lighter."

"You need to get your mind off your work," she said.

"I know." I shook it off. "It's not my job."

But my job had a way of nagging at me, and that night, I dreamed we were there in that very restaurant, with that same waiter, and when he handed me the bill, he said, "You know what happened wasn't right. Look at all the casualties."

And instead of drinks and entrees, the receipt showed a list of names:

Karl Larsson

Cade Weller

Nazari Khan

I woke up around 3:00 a.m. thinking about that. All three were related to the case I'd been working on, and all were casualties of some sort. Larsson and Weller were dead, both from opioids, I might add. And Nazari Khan, the reporter who'd been sounding the death knell of Graham's company, had wrecked his career by adamantly reporting a set of facts that was completely wrong.

By 3:30 a.m., I had moved to the desk by the window while Claire slept in the bed behind me. I muted the sound on my laptop, but the light of the monitor woke her up.

"Freddy!" She was sleepy and irritated. "Turn that off."

"I just want to see something."

"Stop working!" Her voice had a plaintive note.

"Just this one car," I said.

I plugged in the thumb drive Jim Burkheim had given me, the one of the cars passing in front of the little brick house near Larsson's office the night of the disappearance, ghostly silhouettes drifting silently through silver fog.

Though it was impossible to tell the make or model of any of them, one stood out. It passed around 10:30, heading toward the office, and then returned two hours later, going the other way, one light pointing down at the road, the other straying upward, illuminating the fog.

"Claire," I said softly.

"What?" She was annoyed.

"Nazari Khan lives in New York, right?"

"Ugh..." Exasperated sigh. "Freddy!"

"Right?"

"Freddy, please turn that off. Come back to bed."

25

He lived near Gramercy Park. I sent a message through the contact page on his website at 3:48 a.m. and he responded at 7:00. My message said I'd been investigating Larsson's disappearance and I asked if he'd like to talk.

His response said yes, he would. We exchanged a few emails, and then agreed to meet at a restaurant in Union Square for brunch. Claire wasn't too happy about that.

"Freddy! We're on vacation!"

Funny thing, though—she had more to say to Khan than I did. They both knew a lot of the same people, the movers and shakers and Manhattan corporate bigwigs. Claire had known them tangentially, through corporate work in her former life. She'd been in meetings with them, exchanged emails and memos.

Khan knew them because they were key players on his newsbeat, which focused on publicly traded companies and the investment firms and hedge funds that made money off them.

Those two chattered on for so long about people I knew nothing about that, finally, I was the one annoyed. Claire was having a grand old time catching up on gossip while I pushed hash browns around my plate.

Khan was a short, slim guy, well dressed in khakis, a fresh white Oxford shirt, and designer leather shoes. His dark hair was cut short on the sides and longer on top. His accent told me he'd been born in the city.

After his gabfest with Claire, when I was finally able to get a few words in, we bonded over our mutual dislike of Leighton Graham.

"He won't last," Khan told me. "He'll be out of Recursion Talent in three to six months. He's probably lining up his next gig now."

"How do you know that?" I asked.

"He's a turnaround man," Khan said through a mouthful of toast. "He comes in to slash and burn, take the company's cash flow from red to black, and then he gets his bonus and leaves. He's too ruthless to run a company long-term. His management style breeds ill will."

"I'll say."

"He's the bad cop," Khan said. "The next guy they hire will be the good cop, someone focused on rebuilding the company for the long term, with a viable corporate culture."

Claire asked him how he had gotten his story so wrong. How had Khan, who for years had been venerated for his reliable sources and uncanny accuracy, managed to keep sounding the death knell of a company that turned out to be economically healthy and profitable?

He shook his head with what looked like a mixture of woe and frustration.

"My source was wrong," he said. "He—or she—fed me bad info."

"But why would you trust them?" Claire asked.

"Because for nine months, they were feeding me good info. Confidential internal memos that I was able to verify through other channels. Financials that were spot on. Info about initiatives inside the company. A lot of it was privileged information. It had to be coming from someone high up, and it was all legit. Until it wasn't."

Khan dropped his fork and raised his hands and said, "It was my bad, you know? I got too used to this source being right and I stopped checking up. I wasn't verifying the info as fully as I should have been, and I got burned."

Claire asked how he had acquired a source inside Recursion Talent.

"They reached out to me."

"Why?" Claire asked.

"I got the sense this person didn't like Leighton Graham. Not many people in the company did."

"So they wanted to undermine him?" I asked. "By leaking information that would make him look bad?"

Again, Khan threw up his hands. "I don't know. It did feel that way. And the bad news was legit for a long time. But then it turned out to be wrong, so what's the motive there? What's the point of feeding me bad information? Is it just spite? Spite for Graham, or for me? I don't know."

"So you never met this person, never spoke to them or heard their voice?" I asked. "Because if you had, you might have known if it was a man or a woman. How did you communicate?"

"Through Signal."

"The encrypted app?" Claire asked.

"Yeah."

I remembered Leighton Graham telling me that all his top executives used the app. They used it to communicate with each other. That made sense. Claire had told me about cases where top executives went to jail because of incriminating emails that prosecutors had dug out of the corporate servers. If you're going to plot and scheme, why not do it through an encrypted app with self-deleting messages? Then you don't have to worry about cleaning up after yourself.

"He-she also mailed me documents," Khan said. He reached into the leather satchel at his feet and pulled out a half-inch stack of printed pages bound with a black binder clip.

"Take a look at this," he said.

I took the documents and Claire leaned in to read them with me.

"Those are financials," Khan said. "Supposedly the financials for the last quarter, and they're catastrophic. I got those a few weeks before Recursion announced its actual numbers. This is why I was saying the company was going under. Their stock had been plummeting for weeks, and then I got this, and I knew the company was in a death spiral. When businesses like this collapse it can happen fast. Think of Lehman Brothers going under in what seemed like a day, or Silicon Valley Bank.

"I wrote up what I saw," Khan added, "and then I learned it was all a lie. None of the numbers in that document are correct. Recursion announced the real numbers a few weeks after I got those papers. They were profitable again, and I was an idiot, and I got fired. And I deserved it."

"You mind if I hold on to this?" Claire asked.

Wait. Now *she's* interested? Now *she* wants to spend her time thinking about the case she was telling me to let go of at 3:30 in the morning?

This is another reason we get along. We're alike in that way. Give us a challenge and we can't let go.

The numbers meant nothing to me, but they meant a lot to her.

"Keep it," Khan said. "I have half a mind to burn everything my source sent me."

Before we parted, we speculated once more on who Khan's source might have been, and what their motive was, but we couldn't come to a consensus.

Leighton Graham was spiteful enough to want to ruin the career of a journalist who wrote bad things about him, something Khan had done in the past. But Graham himself couldn't have been the source. Why would he have risked such bad press and such damage to his company's stock price when his bonus and reputation depended on turning the company around and improving its stock price?

Graham's employees certainly had reason to generate bad press and headaches for an arrogant and abusive boss. Who wouldn't want to take that guy down a notch?

Karl Larsson was the only guy in the company I knew anything about. He was high up, had access to privileged information, and he was dead.

Did he have something against Graham? I didn't think so, based on what Larsson's wife had told me. In fact, I thought the opposite. He had reason to be thankful, because Graham had hired him into a plum position.

So who, then, was leaking damaging and false information?

26

We took a Monday morning train from Manhattan and arrived at Union Station in the early afternoon. Ten minutes later, we were driving along Massachusetts Avenue, Claire at the wheel, when I saw a blond-haired kid loping along the sidewalk near Triangle Park.

We passed him before getting stuck in a line of cars at Third Street. I turned around to get a good look at him. The kid was picking at his face again, probably from hallucinating bugs beneath his skin while smoking meth. The kid who'd robbed me a couple weeks ago. He was sweating through a white wifebeater in the muggy afternoon heat, his beltless skinny jeans sagging to show a pair of dark blue briefs.

I gave him a good up and down to see if he was carrying. From the front, it looked like he wasn't. He passed us as we idled in traffic and I got to see him from behind. No weapon. At least, not in his pockets or on the belt line. He had probably hocked the gun he robbed me with, traded in his moneymaker for a quick high.

We started moving again as the kid crossed H Street.

Claire was saying something about dropping by the office when I cut her off.

"Pull over," I said.

"What?"

"Pull over!"

"Why? I can't! There are cars—"

I opened the door and bolted. Almost got hit by an Uber before I got my hands on the kid. I caught him from behind, got one hand on his neck and one on his beltline. I hoisted him off the pavement and slammed him face-first into the side of a building.

"Where's my ring?" I shouted.

He couldn't respond. The shock was too much.

Behind me, the cars were all honking at Claire, and she was honking at me, angry.

"Where is my fucking ring, you punk?"

"Dude! I don't even know who you are!"

He was exactly as scared as he should have been. I turned him around and slammed him into the wall again, only this time he was facing me.

"You remember me? You remember coming up to me in my car with your friends?"

Claire was screaming out the window, cursing me. Everyone was honking.

"Where is my fucking ring?" I tightened my fingers around his throat until his eyes started to bulge.

"Where is it?"

He tapped his hand against the hand I was strangling him with, signaling me to stop.

I loosened my grip and he gasped, "Three Globes."

That was a pawn shop a few miles in the opposite direction, back in Southeast. I'd been there a couple of times on other investigations. Things that went missing from their rightful owners had a way of showing up there.

I dropped the kid and would have kicked him if Claire hadn't been screaming and holding up traffic.

When I got back in the car, she was hot. That woman has a hell of a temper. I'd seen it directed at others, and once at me, and it was something to avoid.

"What the *hell* is wrong with you?" she screamed as she hit the gas.

"Turn the car around."

"Answer my question! Are you crazy? Have you lost your mind?"

"Turn the car around. Head across the Hill and follow Pennsylvania Avenue into Southeast."

"You're not listening to me! I asked you a fucking question, goddammit!"

"Claire," I said through gritted teeth. "One of us has to keep our temper and I'm within an inch of losing mine. Do as I say and turn this car around."

I had never spoken to her like that before, and I could tell she was taken aback. She turned the car around—a reckless U-turn right there on Mass Avenue that pissed me off as much as my violence had pissed her off—and for the next few minutes she said nothing because I'm sure she didn't know what to say. But I could tell it was brewing. She was formulating the words, and I knew they'd come out hot because she was mad.

As we turned off Independence onto Pennsylvania, she let it rip.

"Do you think that's cool, Freddy? Do you think you're fucking cool for beating up a skinny kid? In public? In front of all those people?"

"I didn't beat him up," I said as calmly as I could. "If I had really wanted to hurt the kid, I would have hurt him."

She glanced over at me, her eyes lit with fury.

"There's something wrong with you, Freddy. There's no reason for that kind of violence. Ever! It does *not* impress me, do you understand that? It does *not* make me or anyone else respect you. In fact, it does the opposite."

"Watch the road," I said.

"Don't tell me what to do!"

If Claire had a motto, that was it.

"I said watch!"

She had to swerve to avoid rear-ending a delivery van. For the next few minutes, she paid attention to her driving and stewed in silence.

"Take a left two blocks up," I said.

"Stop talking to me like that."

"Just do it!"

She did it, and I jumped out before she could bring the car to a full stop. That pissed her off even more. I burst through the pawnshop door as she let loose a string of profanities that would have made Samuel L. Jackson blush.

Nelson Hayes pulled his sawed-off shotgun from beneath the counter as soon as he saw me. He knew who I was, but in his line of work, he had to deal with a lot of crazies, and I was crazy just then. Taking that ring was like someone had tried to take Claire herself from me, and anyone who tried to do that was asking for a world of hurt.

I was coming at him full steam, like an angry bear, and he leveled the gun at my face, easy and cool.

"You got to calm the fuck down, my man."

I was now directly across the counter from him, three feet away, staring down the barrel.

"Where's my ring?"

"You want a ring, I got plenty to sell you."

"I don't want *a* ring. I want *my* ring."

"What makes you think *your* ring is in *my* store?" He took half a step back. I think he was worried I might try to knock the gun from his hands, even though it would have gone off in my face and killed me.

"A kid came in here," I said. "Skinny blond kid with sores all over him."

Hayes shook his head without moving the gun. "Don't know him."

"Bullshit. Give me my fucking ring before I break your goddamn neck."

"You're forgetting which one of us has the gun."

He took a step to the side, took his left hand off the barrel and kept his right on the stock and trigger. The left hand was reaching under the counter, toward the button that would sound the alarm.

"You really want to do that?" I asked. "You want to bring the cops in here? Because I bet I can find three dozen items you're fencing right now."

"You want to talk shop, Freddy? You gotta calm down first."

Claire was honking the horn outside.

I backed away from the counter, rubbed the sweat from my chin, and said in a calmer voice, "I want my ring."

"What kind of ring we talking about here?" He kept the gun on me.

"Engagement ring."

"You getting married, Freddy?" He seemed happily surprised.

"Maybe. But I need the ring. I got robbed and the kid brought it here."

"Come on, Freddy. You know I don't deal in stolen goods."

"Stop bullshitting me. Where is it?"

Claire was leaning hard on the horn now.

"Describe it."

"It's platinum," I said. "Has some filigree you can only see at close range. Small to medium diamond, brilliant cut, blue and clear."

"Sounds like a nice ring. You must really like this girl."

"I do."

"I don't have anything like that in my inventory."

I looked down at the glass case to Hayes's right. It was right there, shining in its satin pillow inside the black velvet box with the jeweler's logo.

He saw me identify it, and he saw the fire in my eyes when I looked back at him.

"You sure that's the one?"

"That's it," I said.

He took a few seconds to think things through, and I could see he was going to come to a sensible conclusion. He had probably given the kid no more than a few hundred bucks for it. Hell, he could see how strung out the kid was. He might have given him two hundred.

That was less than the weekly bribes he paid to the local cops to turn a blind eye to what he was doing.

"All right, Freddy." He lowered the gun. "Cost of business." He pulled the ring from the case, box and all, and slid it across the counter.

"Make sure it's the right one."

I looked. It was. I put it in my pocket and headed for the exit.

From behind, he called, "Remember you owe me one now! I got a favor coming from you, and I'm gonna call it in."

I had no doubt he would.

When I got back into the car, Claire's face was red with anger. She looked tired, like the emotions had worn her out.

"I'm not even going to ask what that was about," she said. "You disgust me, Freddy. You're like a child. An angry, violent, frightening child."

She said she'd drop me off at my place, and she was going back to hers.

We said nothing the rest of the drive. But I could see her mind working, and I could feel her energy change. I still hadn't told her about the robbery, and she didn't even know the ring existed.

But she's sharp. She can put the story together on her own. I don't go around beating people up for no reason, and I certainly don't pick on random guys who are smaller than me.

She saw me get mad, saw me beat some information out of a person, and then she saw me go into a pawn shop. A pawn shop full of jewelry. She twice glanced at the lump in my pocket. An engagement ring box has a certain size, a size she would know because she'd seen one before. Her last serious boyfriend had bought one for her, and she panicked and ran out on him when she found it.

The first time she glanced at the outline of the box in my pocket, I saw a flash of fear, a hint of that old panic. She kept her eyes fixed on the road for a few minutes after that. Then she softened. She looked again, then looked me in the eye as if to gauge whether she was reading all the clues right.

When we got to my place, she didn't drop me off and go home like she'd said she would. She came in, and she practically threw herself at me. In bed, she was hungry and wild, her desire as hot and intense as her temper had been.

Marriage and children were the two subjects we'd never been able to talk about. Not fully. Not in depth. And I'd never been sure she felt the same way about me as I did about her. I had never actually known whether she'd say yes to my proposal or send me packing. She was as independent and self-reliant as I was, and I wasn't sure she would or could ever give that up.

Now we were in bed and she was wild with passion, her arms around my neck desperately pulling me in, and I whispered in her ear, in a teasing tone, "You act like you're in love, Claire. Are you?"

"Madly," she said. And then, "More, Freddy! Come on. I want all of you. Now!"

She couldn't have pulled me any closer, but she damn sure tried.

27

The next morning, everyone was in the office, all glued to their monitors or their phones in pursuit of a number of individuals. Our business gets a steady trickle of skip traces. A creditor is trying to track down someone who skipped out on a debt, or a law firm is trying to locate a witness to testify in a civil case.

Most people aren't too hard to find. If they're not on social media, they own some kind of property—a house, a car, something that involves legal papers filed with a local government. If a case does come to us, it's not a simple one that can be solved with a Facebook lookup or one of those sites that will sell you a person's public records for nineteen ninety-nine.

These cases usually take us half a day to two days, and we do most of the work without leaving the office. It's boring work, but it keeps the lights on. Today we'd gotten a dump from a local law firm. They were trying to track down six people to give depositions in a sexual assault case that stretched back a dozen years.

Ed and Leon and Bethany and Claire could cover that. A series of nagging questions about the Larsson case kept me from focusing. At 11:00 a.m., I called Jim Burkheim out in Fairfax County. He didn't answer, so I left a message telling him I needed his help.

Then I got in the car and headed for Reston Town Center. Along the way, I noticed I had a voicemail. I hadn't realized my phone was still set to do-not-disturb.

I tapped and listened to the irritated voice of strung-out Jennifer telling me that if I wanted something, why couldn't I just come over and talk to her like a normal person instead of sending someone to beat her up? She was plenty mad, and borderline delusional, probably still reeling in the wake of her boyfriend's death.

I saved the message and then called Jim again as I crossed the Beltway. Again, there was no answer.

A short while later, I was in the garage beneath Recursion's headquarters, taking a look at the front and then the back of Leighton Graham's Mercedes. The front showed what I'd expected. The badge on the trunk told me the name of the dealership that had sold him the car. I assumed it was the same dealership he'd taken it to for repairs after he hit the dog.

Jim didn't answer my third call, and when I swung by the station, I learned why. He had called in sick. Most of Jim's illnesses were self-inflicted and not contagious. The old barley flu. Since it was now past noon and he'd had plenty of time to sleep off the twenty or so beers he'd poured through his liver the night before, he might be in good enough shape for an outing.

When I got to his house, I was alarmed by the overgrown yard, the peeling paint, and the fallen gutter. He answered the door in a t-shirt and jeans. His belt was undone, his face unshaven, his eyes red-rimmed and bleary. Still, he managed a smile and asked if I was up for a double cheeseburger.

Watching him demolish not one but two double cheeseburgers and a plate of fries, I realized that his enormous weight gain came not just from drinking, but from the greasy food he ate to take the edge off his hangovers.

"Why you looking at me like that?" he asked as he licked the ketchup from his thumb.

"You got four months to retirement, Jim. Are you even going to make it that long?"

"Yeah, I'm fine."

"No, you're not."

"I went a little overboard last night."

"You've been overboard for a long time, Jim. You're drowning in it."

"Yeah, maybe I'll take a night off."

"I heard you got picked up twice for driving under the influence. If it hadn't happened in your own county, you'd be in jail now."

Two younger guys, who Jim had helped train, had picked him up and given him a ride home.

"One of the perks of the job," he said.

"You think they're doing you a favor," I told him. "But they're not. If you were in jail now, you'd be sober."

"Perish the thought!"

Jim Burkheim didn't like being alone. He'd been drinking at bars because he wanted the company of the other barflies. After sweeping his second DUI under the rug, the department gave him a stern warning. No more free passes. The next time we pick you up, you go to jail. And don't ever come to work smelling like a brewery.

Since then, he'd stuck to drinking at home to avoid having to drive. But drinking alone was worse for him than drinking with the barflies. I wouldn't be surprised if he passed out most nights in the recliner in front of the TV.

If he'd still been married, his wife might have kept him in line. He certainly couldn't do it himself. And I feared he was right about not sticking around long after retirement. His life was a sinking ship. The department just wanted to get him out without incident. He couldn't do much harm in his little janitor closet at the back of the station, and if he called in sick—which I sensed might happen often—well that just meant he wasn't around to cause problems.

At the end of our lunch, I told him why I'd called. I wanted to talk to a mechanic at a car dealership, but I didn't think he or his supervisor would answer any questions without seeing a badge.

"Christ," said Jim, unsuccessfully stifling a burp. "It's a good thing you mentioned the badge. I left it at the house. You mind swinging back?"

"Sure," I said. "It might help if you shave and put on a uniform." In his jeans and t-shirt, he wasn't exactly the image the department wanted to project.

By the time Jim cleaned up it was almost 3:00. I gave him a briefing as we drove to the dealership in Tyson's Corner. We were there to ask about repairs to Leighton Graham's car. I didn't tell him why, and he didn't ask. His giant, greasy breakfast must have sat heavy in his stomach. When he wasn't almost nodding off, he burped quietly into his fist and excused himself.

Inside the dealership, he was the picture of professionalism. He asked for the manager, showed his badge, and said we had some questions about a recent repair job. Jim's size and the authoritative manner he'd developed over years of telling people what to do went a long way in smoothing out the process. The manager made no objections. He found the mechanic who'd worked on Graham's car and offered him up for questioning.

The mechanic remembered the vehicle. "Silver AMG 55 SL. Nice car."

"Guy hit a dog," I said.

"That's right. The fur was still in the grille."

"What kind of damage?" I asked.

Jim stood rocking on his heels, half-listening.

"Let me show you." The mechanic asked us to follow him into the main showroom, where a shiny black AMG 55 SL was on display.

"Grille," he said, "cracked right here." He pointed to a spot on the driver side. "This faring was busted. That took some time to fix. Owner wasn't too understanding about it. One of these guys who thinks the world's gonna stop for him and then gets mad when it doesn't."

"What about the headlight?" I asked.

"Got knocked back out of alignment. Kinda walleyed."

"You remember which way it was pointing?"

"Up. About fifteen, twenty degrees. It should go slightly down, so the light hits the pavement in front. Does you no good when it's lighting the treetops a hundred yards down the road."

When we got back to my car, Jim's air of authority fell away. It was only then that I realized what an effort he had put into maintaining it, like a vain guy who'd been sucking in his gut for the past half hour and could finally let it out.

"We done?" he asked.

"You are," I said. He was either going to go back to bed or turn on the TV and pop open another brew. He did have the day off, after all. Might as well make the most of it. Or the least of it.

"Before we go," I said, opening my laptop, "I want you to tell me what kind of car this is."

I showed him two clips of video recovered from the doorbell cam of the little brick house. The first was of a walleyed car driving towards Larsson's office around 10:30 p.m. the night he disappeared. The second showed the same car driving away less than two hours later.

In the fog, all we could see was the silhouette. I played the video in slow motion and stopped it a couple of times when the car was in the center of the frame.

The two of us looked back and forth between the silhouette on screen and the AMG 55 SL behind the showroom window in front of us. With its low profile and smooth lines, the car had a distinctive shape. And with a sticker price of a hundred and eighty thousand dollars, you won't find many on the road, even in the wealthy suburbs of DC.

"Yup," said Jim. "That's a match. And with the driver-side headlight pointing up off the road like that..."

"The question is, why?"

Jim folded his arms across his chest and half-said, half-sighed, "You got me."

He fell asleep on the drive home.

28

After dropping Jim off—or maybe I should say unloading him—I gave Cade Weller's girlfriend, Jennifer, a call. I wanted to know more about that comment she'd made days earlier, when she told me Cade had seen a third person in Larsson's office that night.

She didn't answer, and when I got to her apartment, I found out why. She had scored and was high. She let me in after a few minutes of pounding the door, and like Jim, she was having trouble staying awake.

I wonder sometimes if addicts want to be dead. It's a horrible thing to think, but I wonder because they spend all their time and energy trying to get into a state of non-being, of absence and emptiness, like this life was an assignment they didn't want to take on in the first place.

The apartment looked much the same as it had on my first visit, with the floor serving as dresser, laundry pile, dish repository, garbage receptacle, and sleeping place. Jennifer's clothes were strewn about with Cade's, among empty clamshell boxes of takeout, a few beer bottles, and a stained and sheetless futon mattress. Cigarette butts floated in a half-empty Mountain Dew bottle wrapped around the neck in women's underwear.

130

Jen sat in a rocking chair in the middle of the mess, sleepily rubbing her right eye. She avoided touching the left, which was swollen and badly bruised. The split in her upper lip had scabbed over, and the blue-yellow mark on her jaw told me she'd been hit pretty hard.

"You really did get beat up," I said. I stood, because there was nowhere to sit.

It took her a couple seconds to respond. "What?"

"Who beat you up?"

"Fucking dick, man." She spoke slowly, as if she'd just woken up, and she kept rubbing her good eye.

"Have you seen a doctor?"

She laughed. "Dude, I haven't seen a doctor since I was fourteen."

"Maybe you should go."

"Yeah, right."

If she kept rubbing that eye, it would get infected. As soon as I thought that, she stopped. Maybe she read my mind.

"When I was here before," I said, "you told me Cade had seen another person in the office with Karl Larsson the night—"

"Dude, Cade's dead."

"I know. I'm sorry."

"Ha! *You're* sorry?" She ran her fingers through her hair, messing it up even more. "I told him, you know... not to... like, use the needle. I told him!"

"You ever think about getting help, Jennifer?"

"Fuck yeah, man. All the fucking time." Her voice was a sleepy drawl. "You think I'm proud of my life?"

She looked up at me to see my answer, which was a look of empathy mixed with pity, but she was too far gone to process it.

"Did Cade tell you anything about the person he saw that night? Did he give you a description?"

She showed a sudden spark of life, giving me a ray of hope, which she snuffed out a second later with her non-sequitur response.

"Man, if you wanted his phone, why didn't you just say so?"

"You have Cade's phone?"

"No!" She said it like we'd already been through this. "No! I told the guy that, but he went and beat the shit out of me anyway and turned this place upside down."

"What guy?" I asked.

"Look at this mess!" She waved her hand at the same mess I'd seen before. If her assailant had turned the place upside down, as she said, it looked no worse for the wear. "If it's not here, it's not here, man. I'm not going to lie to you."

Talking to a person in her condition takes a lot of patience, sometimes more than I have. Still, I kept it together, kept a calm, even tone.

"Who beat you up?"

"Your friend."

"What friend?"

"Your investigator friend. The guy you went over and talked to across the street the last time you were here."

Explorer Guy? My friend? I busted the guy's window out with his own head, and he nearly murdered me with an injection of heroin or fentanyl or whatever it was that sent me up into the clouds before putting me to sleep.

How could she think we were friends?

I remembered she wasn't too clear-headed on that visit. And she shut the door before me and Explorer Guy got into it, so maybe she didn't see the fight. Still, I wanted to make sure we were talking about the same person.

"Tall, athletic guy, with a blue Ford Explorer?"

"Tall athletic dick with a fist like a cold, hard brick."

"He was after your phone?"

"No!" There was a touch of frustration in her voice, like I should have been following her lucid and unambiguous account of the facts. "Cade's phone. The Samsung."

"Why would he want that?"

"Why don't you ask him?" she said.

"He doesn't work with me."

"No?"

"I don't work with anyone who beats up women."

"Oh." She looked perplexed. "Maybe he was just collecting then."

"Collecting what?"

"Whatever Cade owed. I don't know why anyone would front him anything, but sometimes they did."

We went on like this for another ten minutes, her letting out bits of information and me trying to clear the cobwebs from her brain so she could put the pieces together into a coherent story. It never quite gelled. The best I could put together was that the day Cade died, Explorer Guy came by looking for Cade's phone, which wasn't there, no matter how hard he tried to beat it out of her.

Then, a couple days ago, a man from the insurance company came by with a check. Between getting fired from Westwood and dying of an overdose, Cade had wrecked his car and the cops had it towed to a junkyard. The insurer wrote it off as a total loss.

Jennifer got a check for twenty-eight hundred dollars—all of which would be going into her dealer's pocket—and a ride to the junkyard to clear out whatever belongings remained in Cade's Chevy.

I was about to leave when she surprised me by standing up and walking to the back of the room. She dug around in a pile of clothing and came up with a cigarette, a lighter, and something else.

She lit the smoke, inhaled a lungful, and tossed me an old flip phone.

"That was in the car," she said.

"Is this the phone the guy was after?"

She took another drag, shivered, and shook her head. "No. That's his burner."

"Why would Cade have a burner?"

"Think about it, dude."

To call his dealer.

I opened the phone to a dark screen. It didn't turn on when I pressed the power button.

"You have a charger for this?" I asked.

She rubbed her shoulders like she was cold, the cigarette clamped between her lips. She shook her head. "Uh-uh."

"What's your last name, by the way?"

"Greenwood."

Good to know, in case I ever needed to track her down. I told her I'd check in on her in a few days.

29

On the way back into the city, I picked up a universal charger and found the adapter that fit the phone. Bethany and Leon were still at their desks, wrapping up the day's work. Claire was at the window, trying to give her eyes a rest after hours of staring at the computer screen.

I left Cade Weller's flip phone charging on my desk and the four of us went out for happy hour. We weren't a lively bunch that evening. The tedium of computer work seemed to have ground everyone down. Everyone except me, who had spent most of the day out and about.

Bethany and Leon went their separate ways around 7:00. Claire and I went to dinner on K Street. We'd been exchanging glances over happy hour, itching for some time alone. We were still on a honeymoon of sorts, after the previous afternoon's passionate romp.

We didn't talk about marriage or the future, or the ring, which she had figured out, and which had set her off in the first place. I think we were both nervous to go there. There was no need to, anyway. Not then, when we still had that glow between us.

She did want to know about the robbery. Obviously, she had deduced that. Why else would I attack that guy and then make her drive me to a pawn shop?

She asked why I hadn't told her about it.

"I didn't want to worry you."

"I get more worried about you acting like a madman, jumping out of cars and attacking people. And yelling at me. I don't like that at all."

"Sorry."

"Let's make a pact. Be open with each other. Fully open. About everything."

I agreed, and then we still didn't talk about the ring, or how long I'd been thinking about it, or when I might ask. The answer to that last question, by the way, was *not yet*. We'd been together just over ten months. When I'd thought vaguely about marriage, I told myself we'd be together at least a year before I proposed. Asking sooner would seem like I was rushing her, and I didn't want to do that.

I had bought the ring only because I'd been looking so hard for so long and it was perfect, and if I had to set it aside for a while before I got down on my knee in front of her, so be it. At least I'd have the right ring when the time came.

The food was good, but we rushed through the meal because we wanted to get back to her place, where we could really be alone. It was like we had jumped back to the first weeks of dating, when the world was on fire.

Unfortunately, the world has a way of intruding. My phone rang in the hall outside Claire's apartment, and I answered without bothering to see who was calling.

Nazari Khan. He was still hung up on the question of why someone would feed him bad information. He wanted to talk to Claire. I gave her the phone when we got inside, then I went to the bathroom. And then to the bedroom. Claire stayed in the kitchen talking and talking and the mood was slipping away.

After she hung up, she spent half an hour at the bathroom sink, doing God knows what. I got so bored, I picked up the magazine on the nightstand and started reading about Washington's premier restaurants.

She ambushed me with a jump attack and started kissing me. Amazing how fast she can bring the mood back.

It wasn't till later that she told me what the call was about. Khan wanted to know if she still had contacts at the Securities and Exchange commission.

"Why?" I asked.

"He wants to look into a series of stock trades. Someone dumped a ton of Recursion stock six months ago and someone else bought a ton right before their earnings report."

"So what does that mean?" I asked.

She yawned. "It means Khan is digging for a story."

She said she'd call her contacts and tell him what she learned.

30

The next day, there wasn't much going on at the office, so I asked Claire to drive me out to Virginia. Her BMW is a nice ride, though it's a little cramped for me.

I wanted to show her the building in Town Center and the office where Larsson worked. It was kind of a work date, though she didn't like me spending so much time on a case that was no longer paying.

"First rule of business," she said. "Get paid."

"I want to do the *right* thing," I said. Larsson and Cade Weller were dead. Leighton Graham had just collected a six-million-dollar paycheck and now, just as Claire and Nazari Khan predicted, Graham had turned his company's recruiting prowess toward finding a new CEO. I learned that from the business section of the *Washington Post*.

"The *right* thing," Claire mocked. "You know, it doesn't hurt to do the paying thing now and then."

"You sound like Leighton Graham."

"You could use a touch of Graham in you to keep that golden heart from going bankrupt."

"Speak of the devil!" I pointed at the Mercedes pulling out of the garage. "Where do you think he's going?"

"An extra-long lunch," she said. "He's already checked out from his job. He made his numbers and got his bonus, and

138

now his mind is on to the next thing. I wonder if he'll step down before they appoint a replacement."

We followed him to a golf course, watched him pull a set of clubs from his trunk and drive golf balls on the range with a fat cigar in his mouth.

"How do you like that?" I said. "The guy who won't tolerate slackers and deadwood in his organization is out hitting balls in the middle of the day, on company time."

"A shining example for his employees."

"You want to see where Larsson worked?" I asked.

"Sure. And then I want to get back to town. We're wasting time."

We drove past the airport into Loudon County, and I made her drop me at the side of a wooded road a mile and a half from our destination.

"Why here?" she asked.

"I want to look at the scene where Larsson's car ended up. Drive up a mile and a quarter, then go left. You'll find the office a quarter mile down that side road. It's an old brick building. I'll meet you in the lot."

"You sure, Freddy?"

"Yeah. Go on."

I followed the Mazda's tire tracks through the weeds and brush. After a hundred feet, the tracks curved right, went another hundred feet, then ended at a tree. It was mostly as Jim Burkheim described. The car had hit hard enough to leave a scar in the tree bark but not hard enough to set off the airbags. It might have been going one or two miles an hour.

I looked back toward the road. It wasn't visible from here. The cop who had found Larsson's car had simply followed the tire tracks and flattened brush until they ended at the car.

I turned around and started walking at 11:48. When I got back onto the road, I called Erica Larsson, offered my condolences once again, and asked how she and the boys were holding up.

"As well as can be expected," she said. Which meant not too well. Then I got to the point of the call. I wanted to know what kind of relationship her husband had with Leighton Graham. We'd been through it once, but I wanted to know more. Some piece of the puzzle was missing.

"Professional," she said. "They respected each other."

"Did Karl ever show any fear of Graham?"

Not that she knew of.

"Was there any animosity or resentment on either side?"

"No. Why do you ask?"

"Graham could be a hard guy to get along with."

"Karl could tune out the worst of him." Then she said something that made me laugh. "Have you ever been on a plane, seated in front of a screaming toddler, and you ask yourself why his parents don't shut him up? It's because they don't hear him the same way you do. They're used to it. That's how Karl was with Leighton."

Screaming toddler on a plane was an apt comparison. I pictured Graham with short arms and short legs and an oversized head, pitching a red-faced fit about his six-million-dollar bonus.

"How closely did they work together?"

"Pretty closely," she said. "Karl was one of the few people in the company who had regular one-on-ones with Leighton. He called the other day to express his condolences."

Leighton has known Karl and Erica for years, I thought, *and he didn't stop by. Just called.*

I thanked her for her time and told her I'd be in touch. In the back of my mind, I had one more question for her. It was the same question I'd be asking Jennifer when the time was right. Both Karl and Cade had been expecting some kind of windfall. Both had led their partners to believe there was money coming in soon, enough maybe to put them in a new home.

Why?

When I got to the lot by Larsson's office, I was soaked in sweat. Claire was in the car, blasting the air conditioning and an old Bob Marley song. We'd been dating for ten-plus months, I'd known her for over a year, and this was the first I'd heard of Bob Marley. There's always some new facet to her.

I opened the passenger door and slid in beside her.

She cringed at the sight of my sweat. Or maybe it was the smell.

"What's this say?" I asked, holding my phone up to her face.

"Twelve-twenty. Why?"

I fastened my seatbelt and told her to drive.

"We're not going into the building?"

"No."

She put the car in gear and as we left the lot, she asked, "What's the significance of twelve-twenty?"

"That's how long I think Leighton will get behind bars."

She turned and looked at me just as I was turning to look at the leafy space on the edge of the approach road, the space that had held the blue Explorer the night I came out here to wait for Lester Tate. The space in which Cade Weller's car was parked the night Karl Larsson died.

"Freddy?" Claire said.

I knew that tone by now. Freddy, I can't read you. Explain.

"You know, these guys who think they're so far above everyone else, who think they're untouchable, sometimes when they're rubbing it in, when they're letting us little people know how inferior we are, they give away more than they think.

"The day the cops found Karl Larsson, I walked into Graham's office and he told me I was done. He told me I must not be very good at my job, because how could I have spent three days searching for someone who wound up being found just a half-hour walk from the office in which he'd last been seen?

"Why did he put it in those terms? *A half-hour walk?* How the hell would he know how long it took to walk from there to here unless he had done it himself?"

I held up the phone again, though the screen was off, and I explained. "The phone said twelve-twenty. I started walking from the site of Larsson's car at eleven forty-eight. That's thirty-two minutes. Maybe Graham really is better than me. Maybe he *could* walk it in thirty."

I was angry and Claire could feel it. She said nothing, just kept her eyes on the road and drove.

I didn't believe Karl Larsson had bought bad Percocet on the street or on the internet. He had died from it, according to the toxicology report. It was laced with fentanyl, but that doesn't mean he took it himself or took it willingly or knowingly.

Graham had been at Larsson's office that night, driving out and back in the Mercedes with the screwy walleyed headlight shining up through the fog. He didn't need to scan in because Larsson would have let him in. Somehow, Larsson was poisoned with a drug that looked like one he'd been taking on his own, one that might not raise suspicions.

Claire was thinking the same thing.

"You think Graham put Larsson back into Larsson's own Mazda?" she asked.

"And drove him to a place where he wouldn't be found for a while," I added. "Then Graham gets out, puts Larsson behind the wheel, and walks back to his own car. A thirty-minute walk along country roads on a dark, foggy night. No witnesses."

"But why?" Claire asked. "What's his motive?"

"I don't know."

"And why would he hire you to find Larsson if he killed the man himself?"

"I don't know."

Long pause, then she said tentatively, "Freddy?"

"What?" I snapped.

"Hey! Watch the tone!"

"Sorry. I'm angry."

"I can tell."

We swung around a wooded bend into a stretch of rolling pasture and wide-open cattle farms.

"Are you sure you're not just blaming the guy because you dislike him? Because you *want* him to be guilty?"

She does her best to keep me honest.

"No," I said. "I'm not sure. But why else would he have been out here that night, and why wouldn't he have told me about it?"

And to myself, I noted that Larsson had died from fentanyl and Cade Weller had died from something like it, and I had almost died from an injection of something similar. I still hadn't told Claire about that, and I didn't want to. If she worried as much about me as I did about her, she'd ask me to find a new job.

The similarity of the two deaths, and the one near-death, was too much to be coincidence. Graham didn't strike me as a particularly imaginative person. He seemed like the type who, if he found something that worked, he stuck with it.

A few minutes later, as we merged onto the Dulles Access Road, I said, "You remember that article you told me about a few months back? About how the highest concentration of sociopaths in this country can be found in executive suites and maximum-security prisons? Well I want Leighton Graham to feel right at home. Right at home with his very own kind for a long, long time."

Claire smiled, squeezed my hand. "Breathe, Freddy." She let out a long breath to illustrate. "Let it go."

31

We stopped in at the office. Leon was at his computer, rooting out the location of a man who owed one of our clients a lot of money. Bethany was putting together the bills we'd be sending out tomorrow. Claire went through her email, and I picked up the phone, Cade's burner.

It had been charging overnight. I flipped it open, hit the power button, and waited a few seconds for it to come on.

It was a primitive thing with a tiny two-inch screen and icons that looked like they belonged on a child's toy. Funny how a device that was state-of-the-art twenty years ago now seemed so unimpressive.

It had an email program. Why? How could you type an email on that tiny numeric keypad?

I pushed the arrow keys until the email icon was highlighted, then I hit the OK button. The app sprung open and went straight to the setup screen. It had never been configured, never used.

The phone had an equally pointless web browser. Reading on a two-inch screen is impossible. I opened the browser to see if it had a search history. It didn't.

Claire came up behind me and put her hand on my shoulder.

"I just heard back from my friend at the Securities and Exchange Commission. Remember Nazari Khan asked me to look into some trades involving Recursion's stock?"

"I remember." I opened the photo app. Nothing there.

"There was a flurry of big trades a few months ago, and another just recently."

I opened the text messaging app. Empty.

"And?"

"And," she said, "they all go back to two companies. Shell companies registered in Delaware."

"Registered to who?"

I wasn't looking at her. I was still poking at the phone.

"No one knows. That's the whole point of a shell company. Delaware has *business-friendly* laws. If you were looking at me, Freddy—" She gave my shoulder a playful nudge. "If you were *looking at me—*"

I put the phone down and looked at her.

"You would have seen the air quotes around the words *business-friendly*." She made the air quotes, a special encore performance for Freddy Ferguson.

"They're crime-friendly," I said.

"Exactly."

"The shell companies are anonymous fronts for rich people to hide their wealth."

"I passed the info along to Khan," she said. "What's that? Did you get a new phone?"

"This belonged to the guy who was with me when I got robbed."

"Where'd you get it?"

"From his girlfriend."

I opened the contacts app. There was one number in there. No name. Just a number.

"Who do you think that is?" Claire asked.

I looked at the call history. That one number was the only one ever dialed from this phone, and all the calls were outgoing.

"His dealer," I said.

"Are you going to call them?"

"Why not?"

I hit the number. The phone clicked. Rang once. Rang twice. And then, without so much as a hello, Nettie Hernandez—Leighton Graham's agitated secretary—said, "Oh, dear! Mr. Graham is in a meeting. You're going to have to call back."

I hung up.

Claire and I stared at each other in baffled silence.

32

We ate at my place that evening. I cooked seafood linguini while Claire sipped wine and talked on the phone to Nazari Khan. She gave me the summary over dinner.

Two shell companies in Delaware had sold three million shares of Recursion's stock back in February for about sixty million dollars. The same two companies bought three million shares in August for less than twenty million. That was the info she'd got from her friend at the SEC.

"You know what that means?" Claire asked.

We were at the table, and I could tell she was going into a long explanation, because she put her fork down.

"What?" I asked.

"Someone shorted the stock."

"What's that mean?"

"You borrow a big chunk of stock from someone."

"Like, say sixty million dollars' worth?"

"Sure. Let's run with that." She wiped her mouth. "You tell them you want to hold on to that stock for six months, then you'll give it back."

"What's the point of that?"

"I'm getting there! Jeez, Freddy."

"Well don't get offended."

"Don't be impatient." She paused for a few seconds to see if I'd get impatient. I didn't, so she went on. "You borrow the stock, and you pay the person some money for the privilege of borrowing it. To keep the numbers simple, let's say you give them an even million."

"Okay," I said. "So now you have a bunch of stock, and in six months, you have to give it back, plus a million bucks. How does this benefit you?"

"You sell the stock right away. You get sixty million dollars. You wait six months. The price goes down. Way down. You buy back the same number of shares for twenty million dollars, then you give the shares back to whomever you borrowed them from."

"Plus the million-dollar fee."

"Right. Plus the million. But in the meantime, you've pocketed thirty-nine million dollars." She ran through the math. "You sold them for sixty, bought them back for twenty, so you're up forty million. Minus the one, the borrowing fee, gives you thirty-nine million. That's a hefty profit."

"Sure," I said. "But what if the stock went up between the time you sold it and when you bought it back? You'd lose."

"You would." She picked up a prawn with her fork.

"The whole gamble," I said, "depends on the stock price going down."

She nodded and rushed to swallow her food. "That's the definition of short selling."

"Well how do you know the stock will go down?"

Her eyes lit up. She smiled and wiped her lips. "You feed bad information to one of the industry's top financial reporters, the one everyone listens to. His stories drive the stock price down."

"So Khan got played?"

"Khan got played and whoever owns those shell companies got rich."

Now, she told me, Kahn was on a mission to expose whoever had screwed him over.

"He doesn't take kindly to being used," she said. "Or to being shamefully wrong and fired and publicly humiliated."

"I don't know anyone who takes those things well."

"Well whoever did it made a mistake. Because Khan has connections and he's resourceful. He can dig up information, especially when he's motivated, and right now, he's pretty motivated. It's personal. He wants to find not just who benefitted from the stock short, but who was feeding him bad information as well."

"You think they're two different people?"

She shrugged. "Maybe. Maybe not. He's been combing back through his communications, checking the writing style of some of the messages against—"

"Leighton Graham," I said.

She took another bite of pasta and nodded. Then she said through her food, "Yes, Graham. But it doesn't match."

"The writing style of the messages doesn't match Graham's writing style?"

She shook her head. "Not his public memos, not his speaking style."

"He could have changed it if he was communicating with Khan. I mean, he wouldn't be so obvious."

"No," she said. "He wouldn't. Khan is also going back through the paper communications he received. They were all postmarked from Northern Virginia. But that could be anyone from the Reston office."

"If only there was a way to tell."

"If only..." she agreed. "Now let's get our minds off work."

"What are you thinking?"

"A walk. And then maybe a movie. Netflix?"

"Sure."

We took a walk and talked about other things. We watched a drama about rich women in a wealthy California town who all had affairs with the same man, and then one of them killed him, and the others helped cover it up.

We didn't talk about the case anymore, but that didn't mean we weren't thinking about it. Claire and I often tell each other we should get our minds off work, but neither one of has the kind of mind that can let go of loose ends.

We went to sleep thinking about it. Or, I should say, I went to sleep. Claire stayed up long into the night, staring at the ceiling. That's what she does when something's gnawing at her. She lies on her back and stares straight up with her eyes wide open and thinks. I've woken up many times to see the window light reflected on the glistening surface of those deep brown eyes.

At 2:53 a.m., she woke me with a jolt.

"Reality!" she said.

She was upright, alert, running her finger along her lips as she thought.

"What?"

"Reality Winner."

"Go back to sleep, Claire."

33

We were in the office early the next morning, Claire, me, Leon, and Bethany.

Claire said to Leon, "Reality Winner. Remember her?"

Leon nodded.

"That's a person?" I asked. "Is that her real name?"

"She got caught leaking classified documents," Bethany said. "She went to prison. I think that is her real name."

"Do you remember *how* she got caught?" Claire asked.

"Machine Identification Code," said Leon. "The M-I-C."

"Right," said Claire.

"What's that?" They were talking over my head.

"It's these yellow dots," Leon said. "These tiny yellow dots that you can't see under normal light, but you can see them under ultraviolet. They're printed all over the paper, and they use a code that tells you what printer they came from and what time they were printed."

"That's how Reality Winner got caught," Claire said. "The government was able to trace the leaked papers back to the printer in her office. The dots told them what time the documents were printed. From there, they could check computer logs to find out who had run a print job at that time. It was her, and she was convicted."

151

Bethany shook her head. "That's impossible. How could they trace the papers back to a single printer? Wouldn't the dots just tell them what type of printer it came from? I mean, if it was a Hewlett Packard, there are like a million of those in the US alone."

"No," said Leon. "Every machine produces a different set of dots. They're all unique. Look, give me those." He pointed to a stack of papers on Bethany's desk.

"No, wait," Claire said. She went to her desk and got her shoulder bag. She dug out the papers Khan had handed to her at brunch that day in New York, the ones with the bogus financial data that his anonymous source had sent.

"Try these," Claire said.

"They come off a color printer?" Leon asked, squinting at the pages. "Or black and white?"

Claire said she didn't know.

"Because only color printers add the Machine Identification Code. Hey, Bethany, where's that light?"

He meant the ultraviolet. We had a couple of them in the office. They come in handy for detective work.

Bethany found one in Ed's office. A battery-operated wand you could carry in your pocket when you were on assignment.

Leon flashed it on the page and we all leaned in.

"See, look." He traced the pattern with his finger. The dots were arranged in a seemingly random rectangle. Only it wasn't random. He slid his finger down to another rectangle of dots. Same pattern. It repeated all over the page.

"This is some NSA shit right here," Leon said. "See, you can rip this up and most of the fragments will still have that M-I-C. Most pieces can still be traced to the printer. Unless you shred it."

He separated the sheets and shined the UV light on the other pages.

"They're all marked," he said. "And there's a code. We can look it up."

Bethany was already on it. The Electronic Frontier Foundation published a decoding guide online.

Leon looked back and forth between her monitor and the pages.

"These dots along the top left," he said, "are time stamps. They tell you when this was printed. The ones on the right show the serial number of the printer. That's what ties it to a single machine. That's how you know exactly where this was printed. Hey, Claire, give me—"

He reached toward her bag. "Give me a different document. I'll show you. The dots will be completely different."

Claire pulled a page from her bag and handed it to him. He lined the papers up next to each other so we could see two sets of yellow dots, side by side.

"Now see," he said. "Date and time dots on the top left of the rectangle are different. This was printed on a different day, at a different time. And the serial number..."

We were all leaning in now to see.

"Hey, Bethany, get me a—"

She handed him a magnifying glass before he could finish his sentence. He moved it back and forth between the two documents so we all could see.

"The serial number on the right side of the rectangle..." He hesitated, not sure if what he was seeing was right. But we all saw it.

"Is the same," Bethany said.

I looked at the words on the second document. It was the AI profile of Claire that Tony Nguyen had printed for me the day I interviewed him in Karl Larsson's office. Nazari Khan's source was sending phony information from that same printer in that same office.

Claire stared at me, wide-eyed. She got it right away.

I had to explain it to Bethany and Leon.

34

Jennifer Greenwood didn't answer when I called, so I picked up a cheap Android phone at Target and drove out to her place.

She didn't answer when I knocked, but the door was unlocked. I pushed it open. It was too dark to see clearly. In the dim light, I could only make out vague shapes on the floor, piles of clothing and garbage.

"Jennifer?"

No response.

"Jennifer, are you in here?"

I pushed the door open all the way. That gave enough light to see a little better. The place was such a mess, I thought I'd have to sift through the piles of junk one by one until I found her. If she was even there.

A whimper and a sob told me she was. The sound came from the rear left corner of the room. I found the light switch and flipped it on. An overpowered LED light on the ceiling lit the room with a harsh blue-white light.

She was on the futon, in the corner in back, curled in a ball, quietly sobbing.

I stood beside her, and she whispered, "I'm so sick, Freddy. I'm so, so sick!"

She was pale. Her eyes were watering and her nose was running. I knelt and felt her forehead. She was hot and sweaty, her breathing shallow and quick. I felt her pulse. It was through the roof, like she'd just completed the sprint of her life.

"Do you have fifty dollars?" she pleaded.

She was dopesick.

"I'm not giving you money to get high."

"I'll suck your—"

I clapped my hand over her mouth. "Don't talk like that. Don't you ever talk like that."

When I removed my hand, she said, "I mean it, Freddy."

"That's just the illness talking."

"You don't know what it feels like. Freddy, I want to die. Help me out, or I'm going to die. Please!"

"You're going to die like Cade did, with a needle in your arm."

"That's fine," she said. "As long as I get a hit. Every bone in my body hurts."

"Come on," I said.

"Come where? I can't get up."

I lifted her from the filthy futon mattress and she howled.

"Don't touch me! Don't move me. That hurts!"

"You asked me to help you."

I carried her to the car and drove to Virginia Hospital Center in Arlington. She was whimpering at the start of the ride, and then she started retching. I didn't really get scared until her arm curled up and she started screaming.

"What the hell's wrong with your arm? Why's it doing that?"

I was trying to keep my eyes on her and the road.

"Ow, God! It's cramping."

I've never seen a person so miserable. I hit the gas and ran a few yellow lights to get her to the ER as fast as possible.

I carried her in. She wasn't going to die, even if she felt like she was.

While the staff got her checked in and stabilized, I called an addiction treatment hotline and told them her story. They put me in touch with someone who'd come by as soon as possible, a former addict four years clean.

The check-in and the calls took a little over an hour. Next time I saw Jennifer, she was on a bed in the back of the ER, still looking pale and ill, but no longer in agony. I assumed they'd given her methadone, or something like it, to take away the worst of the sickness.

"How are you feeling?" I asked.

"I don't want to be here." Her face had a pouty look.

"You don't want to be anywhere."

"Why did you bring me here?"

"You asked me to help you."

"I asked you to help me get high."

"Yeah, you remember what you said to me? What you were willing to do to get high?"

That put some color in her cheeks.

"I was desperate, okay?" Though her voice was barely a whisper, I could hear the shame in it.

"And that's how you want to live?"

She shook her head and her eyes teared up. "You don't get it, Freddy. There's no way out of this."

"Someone's coming in to talk to you. Someone who's been where you are now, who's four years clean."

Again she shook her head, and then turned her face to the wall. "I've talked to lots of people like that. It doesn't work."

"Well try," I said. "That's all anyone can do in this life. Try."

To my surprise, that made her smile.

"What's funny?" I asked.

"I'm used to getting lectured. You know, the hard sell. Quit now or die. I like your approach better. Trying sounds a lot easier than having to succeed on pain of death."

"Hey, I wanted to ask you something."

"What?"

I pulled out the cheap Android phone I'd bought at Target. I had already started it up and gone through the initial setup screens. Now it was asking for a Google account. I had come out here on a gamble, with no guarantee it would work, but I had to try.

"You know Cade's Gmail address?"

Turns out she did. I typed it in.

"And his password?"

That brought another smile. "Jennifer," she said. "Plus my birth year. It was the only thing he could remember, besides his own name."

"Capital J?"

She shrugged. "Capital J and then a three instead of an E."

"And what year were you born?"

"Nineteen ninety-eight."

J3nnifer1998. The sign-in worked, and then—dammit! Then it said, "Please enter the code we sent to your registered Android device."

Registered Android device? That would be Cade's old phone. The one that was missing. Nobody knew where that was, not even the guy in the blue Explorer. If he had known, he wouldn't have come by Jennifer's place looking for it.

My hope was to unlock the phone and restore all the contents, just as I'd done with my own new phone after getting robbed. If Cade had backed his phone up to the cloud, I would have been able to get everything.

Now that hope was dashed.

I was going to leave, but Jennifer asked me to stay until the guy from the addiction treatment center arrived. She held on to my arm the same way my son Lenny used to when he was three. I'd tuck him into bed, and he would grab me and say, "Don't go." He'd ask me to tell him a story, which is kind of what Jennifer started doing, in her own, less innocent way. She wanted to hear stories about me.

"You ever use drugs, Freddy?"

"No."

"Drink?"

"Not much."

"Whore?"

"No."

"What do you do for fun?"

"I rescue damsels in distress."

"You have a girlfriend?"

"Yeah."

"I bet you're nice to her."

"I do my best."

We went on like that until the counsellor arrived.

When I left, I put in a call to a guy named Terry Tomlinson from the DC Metropolitan Police. I'd met him on a case a few years back, and he'd become a valuable contact.

"What's up, Freddy?"

"I was wondering if you could do me a favor."

"Depends what it is."

"A kid named Cade Weller died of an overdose recently."

"In DC?"

"In Southeast. Seventh district. I'm wondering if you could find out who was around when he died."

"Not likely."

"I can give you a specific description of who I'm looking for."

"All right."

"Tall, athletic guy. Mixed race. Looks like Aaron Judge."

"The baseball player?"

"Yeah. Drives a blue Ford Explorer that has a dent in the back."

"You got a plate?"

"I do."

Because the dumbass followed me to the hospital and parked in the damn lot. I wasn't going to confront him again. Not in person. No way.

I gave Tomlinson the license plate number and asked him to tell me who owned it.

He said he'd get back to me.

35

I called Jim Burkheim out in Fairfax and told him we needed to talk.

"About what?"

"A case. And see if you can get someone from Loudon County in the room. That's where the murder occurred."

"Murder?"

I drove to the office and picked up Claire. I needed her to help explain the financial side of this. As we left the city, she told me she had called the Securities and Exchange Commission to report what she suspected Leighton Graham of doing.

"I know the woman," she said. "I reported to her when I was a contractor there. She was floored. You know why?"

She waited for me to say something.

"I'm supposed to guess?" I asked. "How would I know why?"

"She had just got off the phone with Nazari Khan, who had told her the exact same story. The fact that Khan was misled into reporting a series of stories that caused Recursion's stock price to spiral, that piqued her interest. And then I call to tell her who might have been shorting the stock."

Claire told me she called Khan after she got off the phone with the SEC.

"He said he has a couple of leads that could out the owner of those shell companies. He doesn't know if it will turn out to be Graham, but we'll find out."

"Did you tell him about the printer? The yellow dots? That his source was someone in Karl Larsson's office? Maybe even Larsson himself?"

"I told him."

"What did he make of it?"

"He said, Huh!"

"That was it?"

"That was it," she said.

When we reached the highway, we ran through our story. It would have to be tight to get three different counties to put cops on the case.

"Three counties?" Claire asked. "Fairfax, Loudon, and who?"

"Arlington."

"How do they fit in?"

"Someone's following Cade Weller's girlfriend." Or me. He may have been following me. I didn't say it, because I didn't want Claire to worry.

"Who is he?" she asked.

"That's sexist," I teased. "Just because someone's stalking a young woman, you assume he's a guy?"

"Stop goofing around."

"I don't know who he is. But I want a guard on her. I want her protected."

When we got to the Reston station, we found Jim Burkheim and four other cops waiting for us in a conference room. Two of the others were from Fairfax: a sergeant and a captain. The other two, both detectives, were from Loudon. Apparently, they were taking this seriously. The pressure was on for Claire and me to make a case, to not look like fools for wasting their time.

It took us thirty minutes to lay it all out, and we got a little boost along the way. Claire's phone chimed with a message from her friend in the SEC. She was assigning an investigator to look into the trading allegations. If the feds were taking this seriously, so could the counties of Northern Virginia.

The Loudon cops said they'd take another look at Karl Larsson's death. Fairfax said they'd put a watch on Leighton Graham, because if any of this was true, he might try to bail sometime soon—especially if he felt any pressure coming down.

"You didn't do anything to tip your hand, did you, Freddy?"

That was Jim Burkheim talking.

I shook my head. "I haven't had any contact with Graham since he let me go. The guy thinks I'm an idiot, thinks he's smarter than literally everyone. I'm content to let him go on thinking that. Now what about Arlington? What about a guard for Jennifer Greenwood?"

The Fairfax captain said he'd arrange it. They'd put out a bulletin on the blue Explorer as well. If Claire hadn't been there, I would have told them about my encounter with the driver of that Explorer, how the guy almost killed me. I made a mental note to call Burkheim later and fill him in.

"And the phone," I said. "I'm still not sure what to do about Cade's missing phone."

Because everything hinged on that.

"Leave it to me," said Burkheim. And I could see a light in his eye that hadn't been there for months. The light of a cop who thinks he has something big in his net.

36

The next day, I got a call from Erica Larsson. She asked if I could come by. Jim Burkheim had visited her that morning and talked a little too liberally. She didn't know the whole story, not as I had laid it out to the cops, but she knew the cops now thought her husband might have been murdered. They had asked for permission to exhume his remains for a second autopsy.

When I got there, her sons were in the kitchen making sandwiches. Two thickset, well-mannered college kids who had their father's blue eyes. They each said a polite hello and shook my hand. Then they cleared out. Took their sandwiches upstairs to their rooms, so their mom could talk to me alone.

She didn't waste any time. She asked me into the living room, sat beside me on the couch, and said softly, "They're digging him up."

I wanted to say something comforting, but what do you say in a situation like this?

"The police now think Karl may not have overdosed. I mean, may not have eaten the pill. I mean... Oh, I don't know what I mean."

"They think someone else may have drugged him."

"That's what I mean. I think. Oh, God, we just buried him a week ago. What could they be looking for?"

A puncture, perhaps? A place where a needle went in?

I wasn't going to say it. There was no use speculating, and whether my guess was correct or not, it would not have comforted her.

She took a deep breath, gathered herself, and said, "I don't want to waste your time, Freddy. But I did want to pass something along, because now that it looks like there might be a crime involved, this may be relevant."

I could tell whatever she had to say made her deeply uncomfortable. She kept taking big breaths, like she was about to begin, and she kept losing her nerve. When she looked into my eyes for reassurance, I gave her all I could. Finally, she began.

"You know Leighton and Karl worked together before?"

"In California," I said.

"They worked at a startup. Actually, it was beyond the startup phase at that point. They had close to a thousand people on staff, and they had just closed a Series C. Do you know what that is?"

I shook my head.

"It's a round of funding given to companies that have proven they have a viable product and a real market. The Series C is a cash infusion that gives them money to expand. It buys them time to grow without having to worry about short-term profits."

I nodded and said okay.

"The investors installed Leighton Graham to run the company at that point. It was part of the conditions of the funding. He was known for running a tight ship, for being efficient and focused and not tolerating waste."

I noticed she didn't mention his people skills.

"Karl had been at the company for a year by then."

"Was this before or after his accident?" I asked. Meaning the accident that had left them struggling under a lifetime of debt.

"After," she said. "Leighton promoted him, and the two of them worked quite closely. Two years later, the company went under. Those gambles don't always pay off. Among tech companies, it's often winner take all. If you don't get enough market share, you either get bought out or you go under. They went under.

"The investors sold off some of the company's core technology, but other than that, there was nothing of value remaining."

She paused and smoothed her slacks. "I'm sorry, Freddy. I should have offered you something to drink. Would you like some coffee? Or water?"

"No, thank you. Go on."

"There's a cleanup process when a company dies. They have to close out the books. And when they did that..."

She paused again. This was the hard part.

"They found over a million dollars had gone missing. The investors pointed the finger at Leighton Graham. How could that money disappear under the leadership of someone who ran such a tight ship? He had to have known about it. He had to be in on it. But their investigation turned up no evidence."

She swallowed hard and added, "Against Leighton. It did, however, cast suspicion on Karl. That became another stress on our marriage. He was eventually cleared for lack of evidence. In the end, the investors felt that Leighton or Karl or both of them had gotten away with a crime. Leighton hired a lawyer every bit as nasty as himself to threaten all the investors with a libel suit if they ever publicly mentioned their suspicions. Their unproven suspicions.

"So they swept it under the rug. Those investors deal in billions. They didn't lose sleep over one and a half million, even if it did make them angry. But their whisper network ensured Leighton would never again run a company in the Valley. That's why he's now on this side of the country."

I told her I was surprised anyone would hire him after that.

"Are you?" she asked. "I'm not. Look at these men who get away with crimes year in and year out and are never held to account. When you get up to certain level of wealth, it's like you have a free pass. You can do whatever you want, and the boys in the millionaires' club will look out for you. Especially if they think you're useful, if they think you can bring in more money for them.

"The thing I want you to know about all this..." And here, she closed her eyes.

"The thing I want you to know is that Leighton did steal the money." She opened her eyes. "He used Karl to do it. Karl had full access to all of the company's systems, and he had the technical savvy to move money and alter digital records without anyone finding out.

"We got three hundred thousand dollars out of that, Karl and I. We used it to pay off our legal bills. We still had the medical bills and the house and the two judgments against us from Karl's accident. But three hundred thousand took one creditor off our backs for good.

"Now, I'm sorry to have to bring this up, especially now that Karl is gone. But I wanted you to know. I wanted you to know, because..."

She finally lost it, put her hand to her mouth, and started sobbing.

"Because Karl had been talking about money coming in. Because he was telling me we were going to move to a better house. Because Leighton picked him, Leighton *chose* him for that job, and now that he's dead, I think they may have been up to something. I think if Karl really was murdered, you should know where to look. You should... That man is mean, and he is low. After the startup collapsed, he managed to intimidate all the investors out in California, and you can't do that with just bluffs. The people you're intimidating can sense whether or not you're going to follow through on your threats, and Leighton has the kind of malice that makes you fear him."

This was evidence. Testimony from a credible character witness who had known the man personally for years.

I asked her if she'd be willing to repeat her story to the police. She feared telling the part about Karl receiving three hundred thousand in stolen money. She feared ruining her sons' high opinion of their father. She worried the investors would try to claw back the money.

I told her she should think about it. She didn't have to decide now. She could wait to see if the second autopsy revealed any evidence of homicide. And then she would have a tough choice to make. Testify, and ruin her late husband's reputation, taint her sons' memory of their dad, and fall deeper into debt. Or risk letting her husband's killer walk.

The last thing she asked me before I left was, "Why did Leighton hire you? If he killed my husband—and I can't imagine who else would—why would he hire a detective to investigate?"

I knew the answer to that, but I couldn't tell her. I was still waiting on the evidence that would make or break the case, and I thought there was only a fifty-fifty chance of it coming through.

37

When I walked into the office that afternoon, Bethany looked up from her monitor with a huge smile.

"What?" I asked. I looked over at Leon to see if he was in on this too. As usual, he was in his own world, playing a video game on his work computer.

"Claire will tell you."

"Claire will tell me what?"

Bethany rolled her eyes. "Well if I tell you then that'll ruin Claire telling you."

"Just tell me!"

"No!" Now she was scowling.

I walked to my desk and was about to check my email when I got a call from Terry Tomlinson from the Metropolitan Police.

"Your blue Explorer," he said, "belongs to a guy from Springfield, Virginia, named Ray Rollins."

"He have a record?"

"Arrests. No convictions."

"Arrests for what?"

"Possession and prostitution."

"Prostitution?" I said. "Like, he got caught picking someone up?"

"Like, he got caught selling favors. For an agency, actually."

"Who was paying him?"

"A person I cannot name."

"A man?"

"A man."

If Tomlinson couldn't say the name, it was probably a congressman or someone high up in government. One of the perks of power. Your name gets wiped from the record.

"What about the possession charge?" I asked. "What was he carrying?"

"Fentanyl. And he was using it too. The cop who brought him in said the guy had tracks on his arm. That's roulette right there. Mismeasure heroin, you might be okay. Fentanyl, no. Now, tell me what you know about him, Freddy."

"Hold on."

I went into Ed's office and shut the door. Ed was in there, sitting behind his desk, chin in hand, reading from the computer monitor. I put my finger to my lips, asking him to be quiet. He nodded.

I didn't want Bethany or Leon to hear this story, because it would get back to Claire. I'd tell her once the case was closed, but not now.

I said to Tomlinson, "Sorry, Terry. I should have told you this the first time I called, in case someone from Metro PD tried to pull him over. This guy is dangerous. I got in a fight with him the other day and he stuck me with a needle. Put me out for hours."

Ed raised an eyebrow.

Tomlinson asked what was in the needle.

"Some kind of opioid, I think. Maybe fentanyl."

"If it was fentanyl, you'd be dead."

"I'd be dead if the needle hadn't broken off. He stuck my forearm while I was driving my fist through his skull. I'm telling you this because your guys need to be careful with him."

"All right," he said. "Thanks for the heads-up. Now I got one more thing for you."

"Shoot."

"We got a witness in Southeast who says Cade Weller OD'd inside a blue Ford Explorer. He didn't say anything about a dent in the back, but Weller was in the passenger seat and the driver just pushed him out onto the sidewalk and took off.

"Another thing," Tomlinson added. "The Explorer wasn't a car they were used to seeing. They get some regulars down there. And another thing too, Weller didn't have any money. He'd been robbed the day before, and he was begging people to front him. No one was giving him anything. Then the Candyman came along in his blue Ford and must have given him just what he was after."

We chatted for another minute before ending the call. Tomlinson said Metro would keep an eye out for the Explorer, especially now that Fairfax had a bulletin out, but with no solid evidence linking it to a crime, it wouldn't be a high priority target. Unless I wanted to make a statement about my encounter with the driver. I told him I'd think about that.

Ed's eyebrow was still raised when I got off the phone.

"What kind of trouble are you getting into now, Freddy?"

I filled him in on the details of the case, telling him everything I'd told Jim Burkheim the day before, plus my conversation with Erica.

None of it seemed to move him. He listened impassively with his head leaning against his fist, and when I was all done, he said, "Who's paying for all this work?"

"No one."

He shook his head in quiet disapproval.

"When I retire and you take over, which won't be long now, this business is going to go under because every time you get sucked into a big investigation, it's a charity case. You gotta get paid, Freddy."

"You sound like Claire."

"Claire should be the partner, not you. Claire has business sense. You... You're like a dog on a scent, a dog on a ten-mile trail to something it can't eat."

"It's a murder, Ed. I can't just let it slide."

"Let the cops handle the murders. Skip traces and cheating spouses are much more profitable."

38

I walked out of Ed's office just as Claire returned. From the looks of her, she'd been out getting her hair done. I liked the results and told her so.

"Tell him!" Bethany blurted. "Tell him!"

"Tell me what?"

"We need to hire Nazari Khan," Bethany said.

"Khan's a reporter, not a detective. Tell me what, Claire?"

"Reporters can be detectives," she said.

The stylist had taken a couple inches off her hair and put a little wave in it. She really did look good.

"Spill it," I told her.

"These shell companies are impossible to crack," she said. "By most normal means. But Khan knows how they work, and when he digs for information, he doesn't use normal means. He uses any means."

She explained that shell companies are typically registered in Delaware, that you need to hire a lawyer to file the papers, and you need to register a business address to receive legal papers, tax documents, and other official communications.

A huge number of shell companies are registered to a handful of addresses. One building in Wilmington is home to thousands of them, including the two that were trading in Recursion's stock.

Khan figured out which lawyer had filed the papers for those companies, then he drove from New York to Wilmington and started snooping around. Turns out this lawyer recently let go of a staff member. Turns out this staff member didn't have warm feelings for his former boss. Said staffer didn't much like Leighton Graham either. Not after their encounter in the lawyer's office. Graham had driven up there late last year to meet in person.

Nazari Khan spent twenty-five hundred dollars of his own money to get hard evidence from the guy showing Graham had set up the shell companies.

"Those corporate filings are mostly boilerplate," Claire said. "Lawyers don't waste time on that. Their paralegals will put together the basic documents, then the lawyer and client review them and make changes."

The disgruntled staffer had sat in on the meeting in which Graham asked for changes, and had an original draft of the filing, marked up with blue ink in both the lawyer's and Graham's handwriting.

In fact, he had stolen a trove of similar drafts incriminating dozens of other rich people who wanted to hide their money, and he let Khan know that all his stolen papers were for sale to the highest bidder.

One of the things I've learned during my years as an investigator is that crooked people tend to work with other crooked people. Even if an employee comes on board as a straight arrow, the ethics of the business will rub off on them if they stick around long enough. They see the guy they're working for makes big money skirting the law, or outright breaking it, so why should they be the simp and miss out on all the profit?

"This needs to go to the SEC," I said.

"They already have it," Claire replied. "Khan's papers may not stand up in court, given their provenance, but they give the feds a solid reason to investigate. If it really was Leighton Graham shorting sixty million dollars of his own company's stock, that's a problem. They'll bring pressure down on the attorney who filed the papers, and they'll analyze every transaction in every account associated with the shell companies. Sooner or later, Leighton will screw up. He wants to have that money in his own hands, so he's got to take it from the shell company accounts one way or another. The SEC just has to watch where it goes."

That gave me hope. I know how the feds can dig into electronic evidence. Not a penny moves through the banking system without leaving some kind of record.

Before we left that afternoon, I got a call from Jim Burkheim out in Fairfax.

Karl Larsson was back on the autopsy table for round two. His car was useless as evidence because the techs and the tow truck driver, who didn't know they were dealing with a crime scene, had contaminated it.

"We did get a print off the rearview that didn't belong to Karl Larsson," he told me. "You know, when a person gets into a car they're not used to driving, the first thing they do is adjust the rearview. Then they forget they did that because it's so automatic. They wipe their prints off the steering wheel and the gearshift and the door handle, but they forget they touched the mirror."

"Was there any sign the car had been wiped down?"

"Yeah, but like I said. No evidence from the car will be admissible in court because of the contamination. Still, I'd like to match that thumbprint on the mirror, just for my own satisfaction."

"Does Graham have prints on file?"

"No. The guy's never been arrested. On another front, I thought you might like to know he's been packing bags. We have guys watching his house, looking though his windows with binoculars."

"You think he's getting ready to bolt?"

"I know he is. He bought a ticket to the Maldives. A one-way ticket. You know why he'd want to go there?"

"Tropical paradise?" I said.

"Tropical paradise that doesn't extradite to the US."

"When does he depart?"

"Tomorrow. Six p.m."

I sucked in a breath. That was too soon. Way too soon. The county cops needed more evidence before they could arrest him.

And it hit me then. I had screwed up. It was an honest mistake, making that call from Cade Weller's burner phone. Cade, who was dead and should not have been calling. I had no idea Nettie Hernandez would be on the other end. That tipped Graham off that someone was on his trail. That's why he was getting ready to fly.

"What about the big one?" I asked. "The nail in Graham's coffin?"

"If it exists," Jim said, "we should have it sometime tomorrow."

39

Morning came, and Jim was still waiting. I asked him what was taking so long.

"Lawyers," he said. "Google usually acts quickly on these warrants. This one got tied up. I talked to the SEC, and they're helping out by bringing pressure too. They don't want this guy to walk. The case is even on the FBI's radar now."

At nine o'clock, Ed sent Claire out to talk to a woman in McLean, one of those profitable cheating-spouse cases he liked. Leon was conducting some kind of electronic dragnet from his desk, some tedious task that an overtaxed law firm had farmed out to us.

Bethany, as far as I could tell, was shopping for shoes online.

Ed called me into his office and asked why I wasn't out drumming up work.

"What do you mean? Like committing crimes that we'll get hired to solve? Maybe hooking up with someone else's wife?"

"Come on, Freddy. You know what I'm talking about. Put your ear to the ground. Work your contacts. We have payroll to meet."

"Tomorrow," I said.

"Why? Because you're wrapped in this Leighton Graham case?"

"It breaks today. One way or the other."

"Your role is done. You need to walk away."

"I'm invested," I said. "Emotionally invested in the outcome of this one."

"So, what does that mean?"

"It means I don't have the mental space or energy to focus on anything else until I know whether Graham is brought to justice or not. I'll know by six this evening."

"Sounds like you're not working today."

"I told you, I don't have the brain space."

"Then I'm docking your pay. Consider today unpaid vacation."

"You can't dock anyone's pay unless both partners agree."

"All right, Freddy. Let's have a vote. All those in favor of docking Freddy's pay, raise your hand."

We both raised our hands.

"Thank you," said Ed. "Now get out."

Jim Burkheim called as I was driving out of the city.

"Come out here, Freddy. I already chewed my nails down as far as they'll go, and I can't drink beer in the office. I need some company."

"Funny you called. I'm already on my way."

40

We took an unmarked car to Leighton Graham's neighborhood, parked up the street, and watched. His Mercedes was parked in the circular cobblestone drive.

"I'm surprised he's not in the office," I said.

"I don't think his mind's on work anymore." Jim peered through a pair of binoculars toward the car. "Ever drive one of those? The AMG 55 SL?"

"No."

"Me either. Wanna know something?"

"Shoot."

"Graham is a chicken hawk."

"How do you know that?"

"We started watching him yesterday. He had a kid over here looked to be about sixteen. Drove in from DC around ten p.m. Left around three. We ran his tags and checked with the DC cops. He's actually nineteen, which makes him a consenting adult. Works for an escort service that caters to older guys with lots of money. I swear, the kid looked like he was in tenth grade."

"You let him go?"

"We didn't even follow him. Didn't want to spook Graham."

I said, "You remember that blue Explorer I told you about?" Jim grunted a yes. "The driver's in the same line of work. Or at least, he was. Got busted for prostitution in DC. Maybe that's how Graham met him. The head of Recursion Talent saw something in the young psychopath, realized he had some skills outside of bed, and put him to work."

"What do you think of a guy Graham's age," Jim asked, "who likes kids thirty years younger?"

"Same as guys who like women thirty years younger. They never grew up. Or they can't admit they've aged. I bet if you asked Graham why he likes them young he'd tell you fruit is best when it's ripe and firm."

"God, don't talk like that. Makes me sick."

We talked for forty-five minutes. Jim told me he had made it through the night without drinking.

"How's that feel?" I asked.

"Like when you forget to eat lunch and you wonder why you feel off, but you can't put your finger on it. But it's this case, you know? I didn't want to miss anything on this one. I was thinking I could have got a call at ten p.m., or midnight, or three. I didn't want to be tanked and miss out."

I told him about Jennifer Greenwood, about leaving her in the hospital, hoping she'd make the choice to get better. Hoping she'd find the strength and support she needed.

"Addiction is an annihilating disease," he said. "I feel sorry for those junkies."

But you don't feel sorry for yourself?

I didn't want to say it. Who knew how he'd take it?

Graham finally emerged from the house. He laid a bag of golf clubs in the trunk of the Mercedes and drove away.

"Can you believe this guy?" Jim said. "Guy kills his friend, steals millions of dollars, packs his bags for the big escape, and then calls time out for a round of golf?"

We didn't follow him right off. The county had a network of unmarked cars to keep track of him. We waited till we got word of which course he'd gone to and then we drove.

The two of us, Jim and I, sweated it out in the car—not literally, the AC was on—while Graham enjoyed a leisurely nine holes. Jim started getting jumpy, checking his texts even when his phone didn't chime.

"No word from Google?" I asked after the third time he checked.

He shook his head.

At 2:00, Graham dropped the clubs back into the trunk, a big cigar jammed between his teeth.

We followed him back to his house, keeping a good distance between our unmarked car and his. Back on the cobblestone drive, he pulled the clubs from the trunk and took them inside.

Three fifteen, he came out with two bags, one big, one small. Put them in the trunk, threw something onto the front step, started the car, and drove.

I asked Jim, who had been watching with binoculars, what Graham threw.

"The house keys," he said. "Because he knows he isn't coming back."

We followed him as he left the neighborhood. There was no point in being subtle about it anymore. He was heading to the airport and soon he'd be gone. This was the two-minute drill at the end of the fourth quarter, and unfortunately, we didn't have the ball.

Jim called his captain at headquarters. He put it on speaker so I could hear.

"TSA's been notified?" he asked. He took his hand off the wheel so he could bite the last bit of nail on the last finger of his left hand.

"You've asked me that three times, Jim. They're on it."

"How many cars we have there?"

"Four. Plus you. I assume that's where you're going."

"And what's up with Google?"

"Still waiting," said the captain.

We followed Graham's Mercedes to the end of the access road and watched him park in the short-term lot near the terminal, the expensive lot that he wouldn't be paying for because he wasn't coming back.

We watched him haul his own bags into the terminal, watched him check in, watched him walk without a care through security to the airline's VIP lounge.

TSA let us through. They'd been in touch with Fairfax County all day.

Five fifteen, Graham was on his third Manhattan. The guy at the table beside him was a Fairfax detective in plainclothes. The guy reading the *New York Times* by the gate where his plane would soon be boarding, the one wearing jeans and a hoodie, was a patrolman.

The four TSA agents at the neighboring gates—two on the left, two on the right—were in full uniform, but they wouldn't raise suspicion because airports always have uniformed TSA agents.

Five twenty. First boarding call.

Graham gets up, grabs his shoulder bag. He's probably flying first class. He's probably boarding priority or group one.

Jim's phone chimes. He reads the text, calls a number in his contact list, and says, "They should be ordered chronologically. Skip right to Sunday night, ten p.m., and go forward from there. Text yes when you have it. *If* you have it."

"They got the account info," Jim said. He was sweating and so was I. One of us smelled. "His contacts, call records, everything."

Five twenty-two, Graham is fourth in line at the gate, the agent in front scanning boarding passes.

Five twenty-three, he's scanned in. Five twenty-three and twenty seconds, he's out of sight, somewhere on the gangway.

Five twenty-four, group one begins to board.

Jim checks his phone, stares at it, as if he can make it ring by force of will. "Come on, now," he mutters. "We're losing him."

Five twenty-nine, the call goes out for group two.

Jim's fingernails are bleeding. He fidgets with his keys, thumbing them nervously like a rosary. He waves the uniformed TSA agents toward the gate, waiting, waiting, waiting for the word.

Five thirty-five, group three.

We're all clustered up by the service desk. Me, Jim, the four TSA agents, and two Fairfax cops in civvies. They keep looking at Jim, the question in their eyes, "Anything?"

Jim shakes his head, looks back toward the VIP lounge. Probably wants a beer to calm his nerves.

Five forty-one, group four, and I have to pee so bad I'm going to let it go in my pants.

The gate agent keeps looking up from her terminal at Jim and me. Her eyes wander to the other two undercovers. She glances at their hands, at our hands. No boarding passes. Why are we hanging around, then? And why the four TSA agents? Why are we all on edge?

Oh, crap, I think. *Did no one tell her?*

Five forty-seven, the call goes out for group five. The last of them line up. The gate agent looks again at Jim and me. Why aren't we getting in line?

Five fifty-three. Final call, but there's no one left to board.

Jim keeps checking his phone. He's sweating heavily. The gate agent looks to the TSA agents, catches the eye of one, and glances pointedly back toward Jim as if to say something's wrong with that guy. You should check him out.

"Anything?" I whisper.

"Nothing." He clenches and loosens his jaw compulsively, the muscles on the sides of his face tensing and relaxing over and over.

Five fifty-eight, the door to the gangway closes.

The gate attendant tries to walk away, but one of the Fairfax cops grabs her arm and holds her back. She's angry. Who does he think he is, putting his hands on her? She doesn't like being manhandled. She looks to the TSA agents for help.

I can't blame her. The Fairfax cop is wearing jeans and a hoodie. Looks like some rando off the street. He flashes his badge. She's not impressed.

She starts to walk. Two TSA agents stop her.

"What the hell? What is this?" She's angry.

And then the chime. Jim lifts his phone, reads the word, and yells "Go!" so loud the gate agent almost jumps out of her skin.

The TSA agents push her to the door. They're all yelling at once. "Open it!"

She panics, fumbles with her ID, swiping it once, twice, three times before she gets the door open.

They push in past her, push past the stragglers on the gangway, and swarm onto the plane.

I hung back by the service desk. I wanted to say hello when they hauled him out. Maybe I was being sentimental, but I didn't like our last meeting, the way we had parted on such a sour note.

And a few minutes later, there he was in his pretty yellow V-neck sweater and designer slacks, the look of shock still fresh on his face, dulled a little by the three Manhattans.

"It was a thirty-two-minute walk," I told him. "From the car to the office. You shouldn't have let that slip, you dumbass."

The plainclothes Fairfax guys each had an arm. They hustled him past me, flanked by the four TSA agents. Jim and I brought up the rear.

I had to rub it in. I just had to.

"You got caught by a guy who never went to college, Leighton. A guy who drives a fucking Ford and has no retirement savings. One of those losers who's spent his whole life on the bottom rung of the ladder and who's—what were your words when you fired me? *Not very good at his job.* Now how's that feel?"

"Ask yourself the same question tomorrow, Freddy. Ask yourself how life feels."

Graham always had to have the last word. If he thought he'd be out of jail tomorrow, he had another thing coming. This was a murder rap, and the feds were on his case for a major financial crime. He had already tried to flee. No judge was going to grant him bail.

41

Back at the Reston station, Jim and I got a look at the video from Cade Weller's phone. Lester Tate had let him into Larsson's building so Weller could retrieve his stash. Weller got high and went to the bathroom. Tate left to continue his patrol, thinking Weller had already gone. He hadn't.

Weller told me himself he had nodded off on the toilet. One of the side effects of using opioids. He may have been out for some time. I suspect he was, since he told me he woke up with a ring around his ass.

While Cade was in the restroom, Leighton Graham showed up and got Karl Larsson to let him in. At some point, Graham slipped Larsson a lethal dose of fentanyl. Maybe he gave him a tablet, maybe he injected it. The second autopsy would tell us more.

Cade Weller left the bathroom and walked into a scene he wasn't expecting: Leighton Graham dragging the lifeless body of Karl Larsson toward the door. Weller took out his phone and filmed it from the hallway. Jim and I watched it in Jim's office, plain as day. Graham grunted and struggled with the deadweight of Larsson's body. He pushed open the door and dragged Larsson through.

Weller walked to the door with his phone's camera still rolling. He put it up to the tiny window of the door and filmed.

We couldn't see Larsson's car from there, or Graham's Mercedes with the walleyed headlight.

Four minutes passed, and then the taillights of Larsson's Mazda came into view. Weller recorded it as it left the lot, whispering in wonder all the while.

"No way, dude! Dude, this isn't happening." His voice was soft and flat, his affect dulled by the Roxies he'd snorted.

He continued filming when he went outside. He walked to Graham's car, got a shot of the empty interior, the broken grill, the license plate.

End of scene.

This was the nail in Leighton Graham's coffin, and he had probably watched it.

He didn't hire me to find Karl Larsson. He hired me to find the person who had been blackmailing him, Cade Weller, who had been calling Graham's secretary from his burner phone. Cade had probably sent Graham a copy of the video to prove he was legit. And Cade, certain he'd be paid off, had been promising his girlfriend that a windfall was coming soon, that soon they'd be rolling in money.

Graham wasn't the kind of guy to roll over for a blackmailer. He hired me to find his annoying tormentor, and I did. I led his hitman, Ray Rollins in the blue Explorer, directly to his target, and then Graham was in the clear.

Karl Larsson was dead and buried, supposedly a victim of bad street-bought or internet-bought pills he'd been taking for his back pain. Fake Percocets laced with fentanyl.

Cade Weller was an overdose waiting to happen. An easy target for Ray Rollins and his needle. No one would even investigate his death.

Weller's missing phone, which had probably been taken by the thieves the day he and I were robbed, kept Graham on edge enough to send his hitman back to Weller's apartment to retrieve it. As long as a copy of that video existed, Graham was at risk.

Jennifer Greenwood's ramblings helped me tie it all together. Why else would Rollins have beaten her? Why else would he have cared so much about a dead man's phone?

When I first laid the case out to Jim and the county cops, they asked why Graham would have Karl feed false financial info to the reporter, Nazari Khan. Why not do it himself?

"Plausible deniability," Claire said. "If he gets someone else to do the dirty work, and that guy gets caught, the boss up top can say he knew nothing about it."

Exactly the setup Graham had used to embezzle from the California startup. Get Karl Larsson to do the dirty work and cut him in for a share.

But why kill him? Why kill Larsson when he didn't have to?

Because Larsson was expecting to get a big chunk of change out of this, enough to pay off a million in debts, buy a nice house, take a vacation, and have enough left over to cover two college tuitions and four elders in assisted living.

How would that sit with the insatiably greedy Graham? This was a guy who had a six-million-dollar bonus dropped in his lap and then *complained* about it. He earned more in one year than I'd earned in my entire life. They were paying him to be an asshole and a bully, something he would have done for free because he enjoyed it, and still the money wasn't enough.

If he was pissed about six million, think how he'd feel about splitting the forty million he'd pulled in on the stock short.

Everything about this guy rubbed me the wrong way. In the end, his arrogance did him in. He truly believed that he was better and smarter than everyone else. He truly believed that those of us working unglamorous, underpaid jobs did so because we weren't capable of doing better. He could never imagine that someone would actually care about the work they did more than the money they brought in.

In his view of the world, such a person was stupid. They deserved to be taken advantage of, and it was his duty to do it. That was his version of the world order. The smart ones up top, like him, were put here to take advantage of the dumb ones down below, like me. For him not to do that, not to exercise his advantage, would be to abdicate. He'd be giving up his God-given privilege to take his place among the little people, the underlings and losers, and that would be a crime. That would be unconscionable.

Good luck in prison, Graham. You'll find a few members of your own tribe, the sociopaths who never made it to the executive suite. And while you're there, you can test out Erica Larsson's assertion that even the devil couldn't get to you. I think he can. I think the guards can get to you even more. Because they're the little guys, and for the rest of your natural life, you're going to be answering to them.

Jim Burkheim asked if I wanted to get a beer.

I told him no.

I only wanted one thing right now. I wanted to relax and put all this behind me. After all the ugliness of this case, I wanted happiness and warmth and light. I wanted Claire.

42

I called her when I left the station. She was in Virginia too, driving from Tyson's corner to McLean, tailing the guy whose wife thought he was cheating.

"He's not cheating tonight," she said. "He's heading back to the house. I think I'll be able to drop off once he pulls into the drive. How'd your case go? Did Graham fly, or did you get him?"

"We got him," I said.

She let out a sigh of relief.

"Oh my God, that's so satisfying! So satisfying, Freddy. Now you can get back to paying work."

"You and Ed," I said. "What's up with you two?"

"Great minds think alike. And business minds look at the bottom line."

"Want to meet at your place?"

"I'll race you."

"You'll get there first," I said. "You're closer to the city."

"We'll see."

43

I spent most of the drive looking forward to the days ahead. I'd take some time off, sleep in late, take Claire out to the movies, go to a game at Nationals Park. I'd shake off the dirty feeling of this case and move on and leave Leighton Graham and his lawyers to deal with the consequences. Graham could stew about it all he wanted for the next twenty or thirty years. I wasn't going to.

Except that Graham's last words at the airport, like so many of his words, had gotten under my skin. It wasn't the words so much as the tone, that arrogant tone of certainty, like he still had the world under his control. *Ask yourself how you feel tomorrow, Freddy. Ask yourself how life feels.*

He simply couldn't conceive of his reign being over, and what bothered me was that part of me couldn't conceive it yet either.

I called Claire a couple blocks from her building.

"You're back, aren't you?" I asked.

"Just parked."

"In the alley?" Had to be. I was a block away now and I didn't see her on the street.

"That was the only spot."

I asked if she wanted me to pick anything up as I rolled to a stop at the light half a block from her apartment.

"For dinner?" she asked.

"Yeah."

"No, let's go out. Hold on... Hold on, Freddy. Someone's asking me a question."

I heard her say "what" to someone, but I didn't catch his response.

And then I heard her ask, "Is that your blue Explorer? Because if you leave it there, you'll get towed."

"Claire!" I shouted. "Oh my God! Run! Run, Claire, run!"

She must have been raising the phone toward her mouth, because her voice got clearer as she said, "Freddy, what's the—"

And then her phone sounded like it hit the ground. I floored it through the light, right into the front end of a DC police cruiser. The impact spun it around, but I kept going, straight down to the end of the block, then right into the alley, jumping the curb and blowing out a rear tire.

Ray Rollins was heading my way, his hands in the pockets of his hoodie, loping casually back to the blue Explorer he'd parked in an illegal spot. Behind him, Claire lay face down on the pavement.

I gunned the engine and hit him. He tried to cut left, out of my path, but I turned the wheel and he went up over the windshield and off the back of the car before I screeched to a stop.

I ran to her and turned her over. He had stuck her right in the side of the neck. The color was draining from her face. She wasn't breathing, and she had no pulse.

"Claire!" I yelled. "Claire!"

I laid her on her back, sat on top of her, breathed into her mouth, pushed on her chest, frantic, mad with grief and terror, as a misaligned pair of headlights—that DC cruiser I had just smashed up—pulled in behind my car.

"Claire!" I screamed. My stomach and back started to knot up.

"Claire!" I pushed on her chest, blew air into her. "Claire!"

Two cops were on me now, two cops pulling my arms, screaming, "Get off her!"

"I didn't do this!" I yelled. I shook off one cop and punched the other in the face. "She's dead! She's fucking dead! Claire!"

More CPR. More breathing.

"Get off her, Freddy!"

Who was this cop who knew my name?

"She's dead!" I yelled.

Now another set of headlights came down the alley in front of us. It lit her face, her pale, dead face. Her pale, blue lips.

"Claire!"

A cop behind me put his nightstick across my throat, choking me, trying to pull me up onto my feet.

"Get the fuck off her, Freddy! That's not how you do it."

Three cops took me down. The one with the nightstick and two who had just charged out of the second cruiser.

I shook them off, all three of them.

"Claire!"

Then Terry Tomlinson clocked me in the side of the head with his nightstick. I'd been hit hard in the ring, but never that hard. My knees buckled and suddenly there was two of everything and all of it was blurry. Two Terry Tomlinsons calmly leaning over two dead Claires. Two bottles of something being jammed up two of her nostrils.

Tomlinson turned to one of the other cops and barked, "Another! Run! And get an ambulance."

One of the cops ran back to the busted-up cruiser. The other called for medics on his shoulder radio. The first guy came back winded and handed Tomlinson a second can of Narcan.

He pumped it in as fast as he could, then hopped up to the position I had been in a minute earlier. He breathed into her mouth, pumped her chest, begged her to breathe.

"Come on," he coaxed. "Come on now, you got this."

But I could hear the panic seeping into his voice.

"Come on, Claire. How's her pulse?"

The cop kneeling at her side, holding her wrist, frowned and shook his head.

"Dammit, Freddy, what the hell did she take?"

"I don't know," I wailed. "I don't know."

"We got more of that?" Tomlinson nodded at the Narcan. The other cop shook his head.

Now an ambulance rolled in behind my car and the damaged cruiser. They could see what was going on, Claire lifeless on the ground, two cops desperately trying to bring her back. The crew bolted toward them like a team of sprinters.

I wanted to pick her up, rock her ragdoll body in my arms, and love her back to life.

I don't remember what happened next. The way Tomlinson described it, I went mad.

It took all four cops, a Taser, and a lot of heavy blows to put me down. I hurt all four of those guys.

This is what they told me when I awoke in the hospital at dawn.

44

My head hurt so bad I thought it was going to split open. One of my ribs was broken. My knuckles were raw and red. Everything pulsed with pain. I wondered if this was how Jennifer Greenwood felt when she was dopesick. Could it have hurt this bad?

And then I remembered the scene in the alley, remembered that Claire was dead. And the pain of that eclipsed it all.

I heard a woman's voice say, "He's awake." A nurse. "Get that cop. The one with the broken arm."

Half a minute later, Tomlinson walked in, looking grave.

"Did I do that to you?" I pointed to the soft cast that wrapped his left arm.

He nodded. "How you feeling?"

"Take me to the morgue."

"You're not going to die, Freddy."

"Take me to the morgue. I want to see Claire."

"You really want to see her?"

Maybe he didn't think it was a good idea. The nurse shook her head.

"He's in no condition to move," she said.

"If you can get into a wheelchair," said Tomlinson, "I'll take you."

I told the nurse to bring a wheelchair. She said no.

I told her again and she refused.

I got up out of the bed and pulled off all the wires and tubes they had attached to me, and I told her if she didn't get me a wheelchair, I would break her neck.

It was a bluff. I couldn't have stayed on my feet for more than five seconds, but she believed me. She went and got the chair and I collapsed back into bed.

A couple minutes later, Tomlinson wheeled me into the elevator. I closed my eyes and we went down. Four floors. Ding. Ding. Ding. Ding.

And then he wheeled me down a long white hall and it didn't matter anymore whether my eyes were closed or open. My heart was broken and the tears welled so thick I couldn't see a goddamn thing.

As a kid, I had taught myself not to cry. Displays of weakness antagonized my dad. Cry, and you'd get a beating.

I never cried in the ring, never cried when I lost a fight. Didn't cry when the mob beat me half to death. I didn't even cry when my first marriage ended, when I learned my wife had been carrying another man's child.

Even now, in this flood of blinding grief, as deep and bitter as all the seas of Earth, the tears could well but they couldn't flow. It's a skill you lose, I suppose, if you don't practice it.

He wheeled me into a room, a bright, overlit room, and he pushed me up against a hard steel rail, and he said as he walked out, "Take your time, Freddy."

My body shook with grief and my head pounded and I couldn't get a breath in. The tears pushed forward and I shuddered, a lost little child all alone in the world who couldn't bear to look at the remains of the person he so badly wanted to hold on to. And then a warm hand reached out and squeezed mine and its owner whispered softly, "You were going to ask me a question, Freddy. It was in your pocket, remember?"

Claire was pale and tired-looking, her voice low and weak. I learned later they had given her four doses of Narcan, several jolts from the defibrillator, and a lot of help from the respirator.

"When you're ready to ask it, I have an answer."

She managed a weak smile.

I stood and hugged her, and that whole river of tears that Aeneas discovered in the underworld burst forth at once.

45

One of the first cops on the scene, the one who had pulled me off Claire with his nightstick on my throat, told me that in my panic, I'd been pushing so hard on her chest they thought I would break her sternum.

When Claire was able to sit up the next day, she showed me the cuts and bruises on her back. I had pushed with such force, I'd ground her vertebrae into the pavement. Her spine was dotted with raw red wounds.

Tomlinson said if the fentanyl didn't kill her, I would have.

"You're lucky Ray Rollins was using," he told me. "Two milligrams of fentanyl is enough to cause respiratory arrest in most people. If he had done his job right, Claire would have been dead. Rollins was using his ammo on himself. Got tracks on his arm and the Explorer was littered with used needles. Dude screwed up."

I asked if Rollins was talking. Tomlinson said no, but that might change when they locked him up. For now, with all his broken bones, the hospital was shooting him full of free drugs and he was enjoying the ride.

"It'll be a different story when he's in jail. When the dopesickness kicks in, he'll be ready to talk."

Jim Burkheim told me the Fairfax cops found Rollins's prints in Graham's Mercedes, and one of Graham's prints on the rear window of the Explorer.

"The print we pulled off Larsson's rearview also matched Graham," he said. "A nice clean thumbprint. We don't need much cooperation in this case. With the prints and Weller's video, the guy's going down.

"We should have dug into Graham's phone earlier, Freddy. He texted Rollins from the airport, 'Do it.' We knew it was a hit, but we didn't know who the target was. Sorry."

Claire and I both left the hospital after two days. Neither one of us was fit to work. Claire kept complaining she couldn't think clearly. She'd run out of energy every time she tried to do something. Putter around the apartment for a few minutes, and then have to sit down and rest.

The headache from my concussion seemed like it would never go away, and the broken rib made sleeping nearly impossible. Every time I rolled over on it, I'd wake up. And I'd stay up for a long time, rethinking my life. All of it, from the ground up. No job was worth this kind of trouble. None.

I thought about leaving the firm. Ed was banking on me staying to run the place after he retired, with him maintaining a minority stake and taking some income off the top to help pay for his golden years.

Leon and Bethany were like family. I couldn't stand the thought of turning them out of a job.

How could I get out of this, I wondered, without screwing the people I cared about? How had life gotten so complex, so tangled, for a guy who had flown solo almost all his life, answering to no one? Now I couldn't make a move without seriously impacting the lives of others.

And what would I do if I left? I didn't have carpentry skills. I couldn't fix cars well enough to earn money. I knew nothing about electrical work, and not much about plumbing. I had no degree. What was left? Painting fences?

Claire once earned good money in the corporate world. She could go back to that. She could earn enough to support us both. But would she want to? She left that world for a reason.

And if she did go back to corporate work, what would I do? Be a homemaker? I could barely make the bed, as Claire pointed out every time I tried.

A week after the alley incident, on a warm September afternoon, we had our first real outing, a walk along the river in East Potomac Park. The sunshine, the drifting cotton clouds, the willow trees and winding river couldn't lift my mood.

"You're brooding, Freddy."

"You don't have to tell me."

"You've been like this all week. When are you going to come out of it?"

"When am I going to come out of it? Listen..." I told her everything I'd been thinking, all my doubts and worries. "How do you just come out of that? It's like, my whole life has to change, and—"

"Does it?"

Sometimes I hate that tone. That utterly sure-of-herself tone that makes you think for a second you must be wrong. It makes me defensive.

I pulled up short and looked at her through narrowed eyes. "You seriously want to go on like this? Dying in a freaking alley? And me almost suffering the same fate?"

"Wait, what?" She stopped by the railing at the river's edge. "When did you almost suffer the same fate?"

I forgot. I still hadn't told her about my encounter with Rollins, the night I spent getting rained on in someone's bushes. I told her then.

"Freddy! Why would you keep that from me?"

"I didn't want you to worry."

"It would have helped when I met the guy. It would have helped to know what he'd done to you. We made a pact, remember? At the restaurant that night. Full disclosure, everything open and honest and aboveboard. But still you kept that from me?"

"I was going to tell you eventually."

We started walking again, and after a quiet minute, she said, "I don't believe in eventually anymore."

"You mean since you died? Since your heart stopped and they had to revive you?"

"Yeah. My reaction has been the exact opposite of yours."

"What do you mean?" I asked.

"I mean, you're thinking about giving everything up so you can play it safe the rest of your life. Your reaction is based on fear, which I understand. That was a scary thing. But do you want to build the rest of your life on a foundation of fear? On avoiding what you're scared of, even if that means giving up what you love?"

"That's pretty much it," I said. "That's what I'm thinking. Losing you once was bad enough. I'm not going to lose you again."

"Yes, you are," she said. "We're all going to lose everything, and the only question is, how do you want to live between now and then?"

Now, I stopped. For the past week, I had been asking myself different versions of this question over and over, but I hadn't thought to phrase it that way.

"You're not going to quit your job, Freddy, because it means too much to you. And you could never work for someone else. You're not the type. You *can* work smarter though. Stop being rash and aggressive."

"When am I rash and aggressive?"

"Why did you charge at Rollins like that the first time you met him? Did you size him up and figure you could beat him in a fight? No wonder he stuck you with a needle."

Jim Burkheim's words came back to me. *You should marry Claire. She's smart as hell. A smart woman will keep her man from doing dumb things. Remember that.*

She turned and started walking again. "You can do your job without bullying people," she said. "And stop brooding about the future! If you're going to plan out the rest of your life, focus on the things you *do* want, not the things you don't."

"I know exactly what I want."

"So do I," she said.

"It's just, the time isn't right."

I had the ring in my pocket. I carried it everywhere. I just couldn't part with it after being robbed. But it was still too soon to propose. We were at eleven months now, still within our first year together. And neither one of us was in great shape, physically or emotionally, after what we'd been through.

"I don't know if there's ever a right time for anything," she said. "There's only now. Right or wrong, it's all we have. We make something of it, or we don't."

I stopped her right there on the path, put my hand on her shoulder, and turned her toward me so I could see her eyes.

Was she trying to force my hand? Was she goading me into proposing?

She wasn't.

I know, because the ring caught her off guard. She was scared, and I was scared, all these doubts came flooding in about whether the ring I'd been so sure of was the right one, the one that told her I got her, I understood her. The one that might tip the scales and get her past the fear of giving up her freedom to take the chance of her life.

I can't remember exactly how I put the question, but when Claire stretched out her hand in the office that afternoon, Bethany took a good long look at that blue-white diamond set in platinum. A big smile lit her face, and she said, "Oh my God, Freddy! For a guy with zero fashion sense, you really nailed it!"

GATE 76
Freddy Ferguson #1

A mysterious woman fleeing an unknown terror boards the wrong plane at San Francisco International and disappears into the heart of the country. Freddy Ferguson, a troubled detective with a violent past, believes she's the last living witness to a crime that has captivated the nation.

Sifting through the wreckage of her past, he begins to understand who she's running from, and why. Now he must track her down before her pursuers can silence her for good.

A modern crime thriller with elements of Raymond Chandler and the classic pulp novels of the 1950s, this character study wrapped in a tale of crime and redemption was named to Kirkus Reviews' Best Books of 2018.

KILL ROMEO
Freddy Ferguson #2

Not since he saw a woman hurry off of a jetliner shortly before it exploded in mid-air (*Gate 76*) has detective and former boxer Freddy Ferguson faced such a deadly puzzle as when he comes across the body of a well-dressed young woman, nameless and unidentifiable, deep in the woods of rural Virginia. In her room at the town inn, she left two mysterious notes hinting at a love gone wrong.

The trail to her killer leads through organized crime, espionage, and the international race for technological supremacy to a seemingly unremarkable man the FBI and CIA have been trying for years to pin down.

THE FRIDAY CAGE
Claire Chastain #1

Someone new has taken an interest in Claire Chastain. He circles her house when she's alone and follows her on errands across town. He tours her home while she's away, leaving little things disturbingly out of place. He may even be involved in the recent death of her childhood friend.

But who is he? And what does he want?

Claire soon discovers that, like Cary Grant in *North by Northwest*, she's caught up in someone else's dark conspiracy, and she has no choice but to play the game. The only exit from her troubles will be the one she makes, if she's smart enough to figure out when and how to make it.

A suspenseful crime thriller in the tradition of Hitchcock and Ross MacDonald, *The Friday Cage* features an exceptionally tough, sharp-minded protagonist who must do some soul-searching in the midst of her quest to survive.

THE REISMAN CASE
Claire Chastain #2

A wealthy business owner asks investigator Claire Chastain to solve a simple case. Is his employee stealing or not?

From the moment she's hired, subtle clues tell her something's wrong: the unbusinesslike business owner, the lingering scent of a woman on the stairs, the rustle in the curtains where someone watches from above.

Claire's gut tells her the case isn't about theft. Her investigation turns up a pathologically anxious suspect, a deeply dysfunctional family, and a murder that she herself appears to have committed.

"If I had known what this case would turn into," she reflects, "I never would have accepted it. No one walks into a burning house."

But she's in it, and she has to find her way out…

IMPALA

After four years on the straight and narrow, Russell Fitzpatrick has a boring job, the wrong woman, and an itch for something more. All he needs to get his life going again is a nudge in the wrong direction.

When he receives a cryptic email from a legendary and slightly deranged fellow hacker — his old friend, Charlie, whom he knows to be dead — he tries to tell himself it's none of his concern. But the guy who stalks him across town at night, the two thugs waiting in the alley, and a ruthless FBI agent let him know his days are numbered if he doesn't turn over the money Charlie stole.

The problem is, Russ doesn't have it. As his enemies close in from all sides, Russ slowly unwinds the mystery of his old friend's paranoid mind and finds that Charlie left behind something worth much more than the money. And no one but him is on to it...

A fast-paced page-turner full of suspense, *Impala* has won numerous awards, including:

- Writer's Digest Gold Medal for Genre Fiction (2016)
- Readers' Favorite Gold Medal for Mystery (2017)
- A best of the year nod from IndieReader (2016)
- An Amazon.com Editor's pick for one of the best mystery/thriller titles of September, 2016

TO HELL WITH JOHNNY MANIC

John Manis, aka Johnny Manic—charming, stylish, impulsive, and reckless—is racked with guilt over the secret he doesn't dare tell. Marilyn Dupree, passionate and volatile, has too much money and the wrong husband. Johnny and Marilyn have a chemistry like nitrogen and glycerin, and that makes Detective Lou Eisenfall very uneasy.

"Poor Lou," Johnny muses as his mind begins to unravel. "There's a madman running around his town, and who knows what he'll do next."

This riveting tale of deception, murder, and psychological suspense was named one of the best of 2019 by BestThrillers.com.

WARREN LANE

Susan Moore is about to hire the wrong man to investigate her philandering husband, Will. There's something not quite right about that detective, but he's all she has at the moment.

"Warren Lane" drinks too much and has a hard time staying out of trouble. He's just the kind of guy Will's mistress can't resist. And everyone is starting to figure out that Will is hiding a lot more than his affair with a reckless young woman.

WAKE UP, WANDA WILEY

Hannah Sharpe has been written out of all eighteen of Wanda Wiley's romance novels. A runaway heroine who won't conform to the plots laid out for her, Hannah has been consigned to a realm of fog deep in the recesses of the author's imagination.

Trevor Dunwoody, the protagonist of a macho action-thriller that Wanda has regrettably agreed to ghostwrite, is single-minded and obtuse, understanding only what he can beat up, shoot, or screw. Like Hannah, he's a character Wanda doesn't know what to do with. When he appears one day in Hannah's fog world, she can't convince him he's in the wrong story.

Hannah knows she'll be stuck in the limbo of Wanda's subconscious until the writer can find a suitable story to cast her in. But Wanda, trapped in a disastrous relationship with the philandering narcissist Dirk Jaworski, is sinking into a deep depression. The pot she smokes to self-medicate impairs her ability to write and thickens the fog of Hannah's timeless isolation.

As Hannah explains her predicament to the thick-headed Trevor, she begins to realize that she knows her author better than her author knows herself. If she can only break out of the limbo of Wanda's subconscious and nudge the writer in the right direction, she can free them both.

But how can Hannah penetrate the fog of her creator's mind from within? The answer is right in front of her in the form of the big, dumb, action-ready tool, Trevor Dunwoody.

ABOUT THE AUTHOR

Andrew Diamond writes mystery, crime, noir, and an occasional comedy. His books feature cinematic prose, strong characterization, twisting plots, and dark humor. Amazon editors named *Impala* a best of the month mystery, and IndieReader named it to their best of 2016 list. *Impala* also won the Readers' Favorite Gold Medal for mystery and the 24th Annual Writer's Digest award for genre fiction.

Gate 76 was named to Kirkus Reviews' Best Books of 2018, while BestThrillers.com selected both *Gate 76* (2018) and *To Hell with Johnny Manic* (2019) to their best of the year list.

You can follow Andrew on Goodreads and at https://adiamond.me.